A BRIDE IN DISGUISE

WAGON WHEEL JUSTICE

BLYTHE CARVER

1

Belinda Salinger knew when she awakened that bright spring morning that everything was about to change. Her sisters were going away, and she would be left at their private investigating agency alone. For a short time anyway.

The year before, Belinda and her three sisters, Amelia, Sadie, and Josie, inherited a successful private investigative business in Sacramento, California from their Uncle Gabriel. Overcoming the apprehension that was common when it came to working with women on such private matters, but with the year 1900 coming quickly, the girls were confident things were changing for the better.

Belinda was the only one left of the four sisters who hadn't found a man to spend her life with. She was looking forward to it happening for her, but in the year and a half they had been in Sacramento, she'd found no one who showed more than a polite interest. She wasn't a beauty queen, but by no means was she ugly. The problem Belinda experienced was that she was often quiet, her nose in a book, staying inside while her more outgoing sisters went out on the town.

So now Josie and her fiancé, Taylor, were taking his two children by his first marriage on their honeymoon to Europe. Adelaide and her beau, Cody, were taking a boat trip for two weeks. Last, but definitely not least, her vibrant sister, Sadie and her beau, who was also the security for the Wagon Wheel Justice Agency, were heading off for an interesting case in Lancaster, taking the train that very afternoon.

Why all her sisters decided to leave at the same time was beyond Belinda's comprehension. She suspected it had just happened that way. Or maybe the ladies thought she needed some time on her own to run the place.

Either way, and as apprehensive as she might feel about it, she was ready to give it a try. It might be fun.

She slid out of bed and got dressed, cleaning her face with the warm water she'd left by the fire to heat it up. There was always a chill in her room in the mornings, so she got up early and started a fire in the hearth in her room so she could get a few hours of sleep at a warm temperature.

Josie was downstairs in the kitchen. Belinda could hear her talking and laughing with Taylor's children, Bella and Alex. She was probably making pancakes with them. She smelled coffee in the air. That was enough to motivate her to hurry down and get a cup. It would invigorate her.

She went through the door into the kitchen and was a little surprised to see the rest of her sisters were there with their beaus, as well.

"I feel like I'm late for something," she said with a soft laugh, moving to the stove to pour herself a cup of coffee from the pot.

"Not at all. Good morning, dear." her oldest sister, Amelia, was the one standing at the stove watching over the eggs in the pan. She poured a cup for Belinda , who leaned in to give her sister a grateful kiss on the cheek.

"Thank you and good morning. I reckon everybody was too excited to sleep late today. So much to do. I just know we'll leave something behind, and I'll have to spend money to get what I'm missing. Not that it would be hard to do, but I just hate to spend frivolously."

Cody, the man she intended to marry, gave Adelaide a big smile. "And that's why you'll always have the money you need, my dear."

"You aren't upset that we're leaving you here alone, are you, Belinda ?" Josie asked, setting a plate of eggs down in front of Alex and moving to set another one in front of Bella. "Here you go, babies. Eat up. We have a long trip ahead of us."

"I feel like I'm tired already," Bella said.

Belinda's eyes darted to the five-year-old, as did every other eye in the room except Alex's. She couldn't help laughing with them. Bella was precocious and sweet. Belinda would definitely miss the children while they were gone.

"No, I'm not upset," she said, putting her cup down on the table and returning to the cabinets to get a plate. She got herself some eggs and bacon strips, picking up a biscuit on her way back to the table. "I'm looking forward to a few days of peace."

"A few days?" Cody inquired, sitting across from Belinda. "And what will you do after that?"

"Wallow in misery and loneliness?" Belinda quipped, giving him a grin as she pulled her chair in so she could sit comfortably and eat her breakfast.

She felt a sense of deep satisfaction when all the adults in the room laughed loudly.

"If you ever get lonely, you know Mrs. Bixby will be happy to have some company if you want to visit," Sadie said, holding her biscuit. She took a big bite and smiled with a closed mouth while she chewed.

"She's right, you know," Larson put in from his place beside Sadie. "She's always asking Sadie to come over and have lunch."

"Well, she's not asking *me* all the time," Belinda responded. "That sounds to me like she likes Sadie. We are two separate people, you know."

Again, laughter filled the air, and having finished her biscuit, Sadie remarked, "She's right. We're actually not very much alike at all."

"I'll be fine. Don't you worry about me."

Two hours later, Belinda watched as her sisters and their beaus rode off in their wagons, one right after another. Not only were they all leaving that day, but they were also leaving at the same time. Belinda waved them off before turning to go back into the office that used up the rooms in front of the house.

She looked at the empty foyer, listened to the sound of silence around her.

She took in a deep breath and held it for a moment. Everything was going to change now.

She could feel it.

2

———

"I'm telling you, Dwight," Lionel Calverson said in a casual tone, "if that bull was any gentler, I'd say it was a cow. I'm serious about this."

Dwight Barnes, Lionel's best friend, threw back his head and laughed. "I can't disagree with you there. Chance is one gentle bull."

"That's why Jimmy-boy didn't put him in with Decker. Decker would have trampled Chance to get to those cows. He'd never have had a chance."

This time he joined Dwight in laughter, and they clinked their glasses together.

Lionel was the son of the mayor of Sacramento. He was one of the wealthiest young men in all of California and was considered to be almost royalty among the wealthy citizens of the state. Not only was he rich, but he was also intelligent, handsome, and a most compassionate man, as well.

Dwight, for his part, was a wealthy man himself. He had a successful cattle ranch and moved in the same circles as his friend.

"Lionel." Both men looked up and saw Sheriff John Nolan and a stranger coming out on the veranda of the mayor's mansion where they were sitting in lounge chairs, enjoying the beautiful Spring day. In front of them was the butler, whose face looked sterner than usual. Lionel pushed himself to his feet and held out his hand, walking toward the men. "Sheriff Nolan and Inspector Binks to see you, sir," the butler finished, stepping back to get out of Lionel's way.

"Nice to meet you," Lionel said, shaking the inspector's hand. "What brings you to our neck of the woods?"

"A very serious matter, I'm afraid," the inspector responded, his voice deep and ominous. He turned his eyes to Dwight.

Uneasiness settled in Lionel's chest as he stepped back to his chair and sat down.

"What's the problem?" he asked. He was running his eyes from Dwight to the inspector to the Sheriff, wondering why the two authority figures were staring at his friend.

"It's Dwight we're here to talk to," the sheriff responded, his voice more respectful than the look on his face. "I'm afraid we have some questions about the cattle rustling that's plaguing our fine city."

"I've told you all I know, John," Dwight replied, looking confused.

"Yeah, but now the inspector is on the case, and he would like to hear it for himself."

"The thing is, sir," the inspector said, coming over to the veranda chairs near the table, pulling one over, and setting it close to Dwight. He plopped himself down and crossed his legs, giving Dwight a crass look. Lionel was beginning to feel even more uneasy, "we've been told that your ranch is one of the few that isn't being hit. But yet the ones around you are. It seems pretty obvious to me that you wouldn't be rustling cattle from your own yard."

"I also wouldn't be hitting only the ranches around me if I was the one committing the crime," Dwight responded hotly. Lionel could hear the irritation in his voice.

"Or maybe that's your excuse," the inspector responded, narrowing his eyes.

The look of frustration on Dwight's face was obvious to Lionel. He leaned forward, using one hand to gesture. "Inspector, we've been over this with the law already. Dwight has. If you pardon my intrusion, you have all been looking in his direction for too long. You're missing possible clues to who it could be because you've been focused on Dwight. He isn't doing this. I've told my lawyer, as well as my father, that this harassment must cease."

The inspector turned his wrath in Lionel's direction, which was what Lionel intended in the first place. He had been friends with Dwight since they were in the schoolhouse. He knew everything that had happened in Dwight's life. It was true that Dwight had left Sacramento and done some traveling, but he'd only been gone seven years and had written to Lionel nearly every day, detailing his adventures.

"I know why you're doing this," Lionel said firmly. He'd been defending his friend's honor since he'd returned to claim the estate his father left behind when he passed on. Tom Barnes had become severely ill with influenza and died within six months of the virus weakening his system and causing multiple other issues to flare up. Dwight had not come back when his father fell ill and did not return until after Tom was gone. Many people held that against Dwight, calling him the prodigal son and judging him for what he'd done.

But they didn't know the truth. Those who did made a personal decision whether to believe Dwight's reason or not. Lionel, of course, fully believed Dwight because he'd been in correspondence with his friend the entire time.

"This has nothing to do with any personal feelings or grudges," the inspector claimed, pinching his thin mustache between his fingers while glaring at the two men one at a time. "This is about catching the cattle rustlers and taking down the boss of the entire operation."

"You have no proof that Dwight is responsible for any of it," Lionel exclaimed, scowling. "Until you actually have—"

"Not so fast." Sheriff Nolan stepped forward, his hands grasping his belt as if it needed help holding it up to his waist. He was an average size man, shorter than Lionel and Dwight but taller than the inspector, who was rather on the short side. "We've found a handkerchief with the initials BT on it.

"The ranch is called Big T because my father's name was Tom. It stands for Big Tom. He didn't have any handkerchiefs made that said BT. Those weren't his initials. His initials were TB. Tom Barnes."

Lionel didn't blame Dwight for being irritable about the whole thing. The law had been after him for the specific reason that many thought he had abandoned his father, who was a beloved character in the city of Sacramento for nearly fifty years. As a teenager, Big Tom Barnes had made his mark by saving a group of children who were skating on weak ice that broke. He put himself in the clinic from near hypothermia and almost died from it. He did lose two fingers as a result. From that point on, he was known as a hero, treated as one, and never used his beloved status for anything other than good.

Dwight not coming home to be with and help his father had angered a lot of the community, and they weren't willing to give him any forgiveness. That included the lawmen his father had been friends with.

"We're going to find all the evidence we need, Dwight," the inspector said in a low voice. "When we catch the men committing this crime, they will name you, and we will bring you down."

Lionel stood up. "I don't know who you think

you are, sir, but this is private property, and you need to leave."

The inspector stood up, too, glaring up at Lionel. "Your father has given us permission to be here."

"And I'm rescinding that permission since this is my home as well. Respect must be earned, sir, and you haven't earned mine. Please leave." He held up his arm toward the door and the other one circled around the inspector at a distance, as if to block him from going in a direction Lionel didn't want him going.

The inspector huffed, glancing at Dwight. "We will return."

"Not to here, you won't," Lionel growled, moving his arm till it was just inches from the inspector and threatened to actually touch him. Lionel wanted that even less than the inspector, he was sure.

3

———

When the inspector and the sheriff turned to leave, they nearly ran into the foreman of the Big T ranch, Mick Lawdry. He stepped quickly to the side and put his hat to his chest, nodding at them as they stomped past. He plopped his hat back on his head when he came out on the veranda.

"Boss," he said, nodding at Dwight, "what was that all about? Same thing?"

"Same thing," Dwight replied. It upset Lionel that his friend was being constantly harassed the way he was. Just ten minutes ago, Dwight had been laughing with him. Now his face had turned dark, and within minutes, he would tell Lionel he had to leave. Then again, it wasn't often Mick came by the mayor's mansion to talk to Dwight.

"Take a seat, Mick. Can I get you a drink?"

"Sure, if ya got one for me."

Lionel left the men behind to discuss the cattle rustling that had been plaguing their neighbors for the past three months. Dozens of cattle had been stolen from the ranches surrounding Dwight, but his had yet to be hit.

Despite that, Dwight's land was showing signs of having been sabotaged in some places. He and Dwight were finding repairs that needed urgent attention where there had been no such emergency only a short time ago.

The law didn't listen to Dwight when he tried to report the suspected sabotage. They didn't believe him.

Lionel went through the double glass doors into the parlor and crossed the long room to the door. He opened it and stuck his head out, looking for a maid or the butler, Henry. It was Henry he saw first, coming out of the den on the other side of the foyer and turning around to quietly close the door.

"Henry, bring Mick a bourbon out on the veranda."

"Yes, sir." Henry opened the door again and went through to the bar in the den.

Lionel looked behind him at the two men on the veranda. Dwight was shaking his head and speaking energetically, waving one hand in the air as he spoke. Mick was nodding and listening.

Lionel didn't have any fondness for Mick. The man was a drunk, a reckless, feckless man. But Dwight trusted him. Lionel had told Dwight of his misgivings with the man in the past, but Mick had never done anything outwardly that could prove Lionel's point about him. Lionel didn't like to make judgments, but there was just something about Mick he didn't like.

"Here you are, sir." He turned back when Henry spoke and reached to take the drink from the butler's hand.

"Thank you, Henry."

"It's my pleasure to be of service." Henry nodded once and turned on his heel.

Lionel went back to the men, setting the drink down in front of Mick. He took his seat again but could no longer enjoy the beautiful day. The arrival of the lawmen had destroyed the good mood.

"What do you think about all this, Mr. Calverson?" Mick asked Lionel. Lionel turned his head, unsure whether the foreman wanted a real answer. He couldn't remember a time the man had put any stock in what he said.

"I think someone is out to get Dwight and is trying to pin these cattle thefts on him."

"But why would anyone want to do that?" Mick asked, pulling his eyebrows together. "Just because of his pa?"

"That's what we've been thinking," Lionel responded. "Can't think of any other reason. Dwight here insists he has no enemies."

"The boss don't have no enemies," Mick said, dragging his eyes to his employer and raising his eyebrows. "Do you?"

"No one in particular." Dwight sighed heavily, his eyes across the backyard and off in the distance. He leaned back in his chair and stretched his long legs out in front of him.

"I did hear some men talking in town when I went to the bank the other day," Mick said. "I didn't think to mention it to the sheriff while he was here. Maybe he should go talk to those fellas."

Dwight and Lionel both focused their eyes on the foreman. Lionel couldn't help wondering if Mick had lost his mind. He should have immediately gone to the sheriff if he had needed information.

"What did you hear?" Lionel demanded.

Mick looked slightly nervous and then answered him. "They were talking about how Dwight went off to get an education, or some of them said to explore, and others said it was because of a woman. Talking about how his father deserved a better son and things like that." He slid his eyes to Dwight and clenched his jaw before he said, "I don't listen to that garbage, boss. Don't worry about that. None of your men think like that. I promise you that."

"That's nice to hear, Mick. Thank you for your reassurance."

"So, what did you come by for anyway?" Lionel asked, thinking about what a coincidence it was to see the grubby man there at his house. He could only hope that some of the dirtiness on the man didn't wipe off on their good furniture.

"Oh, yeah," Mick replied, his eyes darting back to his boss. "That daggone bull got out again and is running all over the pasture. Good for spreading the manure, not good for any person or animal in his path."

"And you didn't get the men and stop him?" Dwight asked, standing up quickly, grabbing his hat from the table and setting it roughly on his head.

Mick jumped to his feet, holding up both hands

and shaking his head. "We have him contained, of course. But the damage that's been done needs your eyes. We need you to tell us what you want done."

"Ah. Well, let's get on with it then." Dwight turned his attention to Lionel. "You care to come with me, and we can have a gander at the damage done by that bull? I'm telling you I gotta get rid of that creature. He's a good-for-nothing."

Mick led the way out the door and to the horses. Lionel was the first to reach his horse. His mind was filled with images of the pasture where Dwight's prize (because of size) bull kept his residence. He wondered just how much damage could be done to anything other than the fence, considering there were no other structures other than the shelter for the bull and the surrounding pasture that belonged to him. The cattle pasture certainly didn't have any structures on it.

Quietly, they rode back to the ranch. Lionel had spent hours upon hours thinking about the rash of cattle thefts that had been happening lately. There were just too many people who disliked what Dwight had done and not enough who could be committing the crime without being noticed in some way. He was astounded that someone had gone through the trouble to get BT embroidered on a handkerchief and then made sure it landed in the hands of the lawmen.

The random attacks made it so there was no way to predict when the next ranch would be hit. One of the nearby ranches, owned by a man and wife with their three young children, had been hit twice. The owners were in desperate need of help, and Lionel had given an anonymous donation to the church that was growing a fund for the family to help pay for replenishment of their supply.

Lionel had racked his brain trying to think of ways to help Dwight prove his innocence. This handkerchief was the last straw. Someone was trying to pin it on his friend, and it looked like he would have to go to extremes to help prove his innocence.

He'd seen an advertisement for a PI business that had garnered very good reviews from past clients. Tomorrow he would visit them and see what they could do.

4

Belinda was just about to go to the back half of the building where their residence was when there was a knock on the door behind her. She turned and stared at the door. She'd definitely seen her sisters leaving. She couldn't imagine one would have turned back in that quick amount of time.

She went through the vestibule to the front doors and opened them both, holding them apart and standing in between them. "May I help you?"

Maybe it was because her sisters were all involved in relationships, and she was the last sister alone. Maybe it was because the man standing before her was the best-looking man she'd seen in her life.

Whatever the reason, Belinda's body suddenly became hot and felt heavier than usual. Her knees wanted to give way a little, but she managed to stay on her feet and give him a smile.

"This is the Wagon Wheel Agency, am I correct?"

"You are correct," Belinda replied, maintaining her smile.

"I'd like to speak to one of the detectives, please. I have a problem I need help with."

"You are certainly welcome to come in." Belinda wanted to invite him to the main office and not tell him the PIs were all women, but she felt it was important enough to mention right away. "I will have you know that my sisters and I run this agency. We are the detectives. They have all left temporarily, and I'm the only one here. I'm in charge. Is this something you can accept?"

Although he looked surprised, Belinda saw acquiescence on his face.

"That's fine with me. Your agency has an excellent reputation, and solving the case is my only concern. Not whether it's solved by a male or a female. Women are often more intuitive than men anyway. You might see things that my friend and I have not."

Belinda was intrigued. She stepped back, pulling the left door open all the way and letting the other one close on its own. The man stepped into the vestibule, taking his hat off and holding out his hand.

"Lionel Calverson."

Belinda's eyebrows shot up. "Calverson?"

"Yes, the mayor is my father. That has no relevance to this case. Will it matter to you?"

Belinda thought it strange that they were talking about Lionel's father, but there seemed to be no emotional connection. It was as if he was mentioning a perfect stranger.

"I don't want any special treatment or favors because he is my father," Lionel continued. "You will charge me the full amount that you would normally charge. It's not like my family can't afford it."

"Come into the office. Let's discuss this at length. I don't know what you need at this point. Let's not talk about money just yet. I might not be able to take the case. And believe me, I won't charge you less because you are the mayor's son. He has many policies I do not agree with."

Again, Lionel looked surprised. This time there seemed to be a little pleasure behind that expression. Belinda wondered if he, too, held different political views than his father. He nodded at her when she pointed to the main office and closed the door when he was in.

He had stripped off his light jacket and draped it over the chair before Belinda even got through the doorway. He took his seat, and she went around the desk to settle in hers. She pulled a notepad in front of her and smoothed out the paper, even though it wasn't wrinkled. Once she had a pen in hand, she nodded at him.

"Tell me what you know."

"My friend, Dwight Barnes, over there on Big T ranch out in the southwest part of the county, is being accused of organizing the cattle rustling scheme that's been plaguing the area. Have you heard about it?"

Belinda wished she had. She felt ignorant not knowing about it. "I'm sorry, I don't."

Lionel took a moment, looking around him. Belinda watched, wondering what he was thinking about what he saw. He spoke while he looked around. "Several ranches surrounding Big T have been hit. Today we had a visit from the sheriff and an inspector who has just been assigned to the case. It's my opinion that both of them are holding a personal grudge against Dwight. I don't believe he is responsible. Plenty of people do. I think he's being set up. I want to hire you to figure out what's going on. I need you to put a neutral opinion in the mix. You think you can do that?"

"Of course I can," Belinda replied with a smile. "I don't know the man, nor do I know the sheriff or this inspector you're speaking of. I can say that honestly because what I've been doing for the last nearly two years has mostly been right here in the office. I'm very good with money and handle the accounts for the agency. With my sisters gone, I've taken the responsibility of investigating."

Belinda could tell she had fueled the suspicion that she had no idea what she was doing. That was unfortunate. She didn't mean to give that impression.

"So, are you telling me you've never worked a case before?"

Belinda didn't know how to respond to make him more confident. She prayed quickly for the right words. "I've done the work back here. I haven't gone and interviewed anyone. But I know what I'm doing, don't worry. My sisters and I all got a taste of field work when my uncle was alive and running this company. For the first twenty-five years of my life, what I can remember of it, I was exposed to the work of a private investigator because of him. He involved us in his cases whenever we visited, which was frequently for me after the age of ten."

Lionel still looked skeptical. "I don't know, ma'am. I heard the reputation was excellent, but it sounds like you are an amateur. I mean no disrespect. I just want the best for my friend, and I thought I would find it here."

"I am a professional, Mr. Calverson. I promise you I know how to get to the truth."

Belinda wasn't actually sure of herself. Her confidence wasn't nearly as high as she was expressing. She simply wanted to work on her first case. For him. Specifically.

Lionel was quiet for a moment, studying her face. She didn't flinch and didn't look away. She held his gaze, hoping she would seem professional to him. She kept her back straight and her hands together in front of her.

He sucked his teeth and pressed his lips together, contemplatively.

He paused for longer than Belinda was comfortable with, but when he spoke, she felt a wave of relief.

"I'm going to give you a chance, Miss. But you'll

need to do some background research, won't you? Since you don't know what's going on with the case?"

"I will do that," Belinda said, nodding. "Thank you, Mr. Calverson. Perhaps you can come back in three days' time, and we can discuss what I've learned and come up with a plan."

Lionel nodded. "Yes. That sounds like a good idea. In the meantime, if anything more happens or there is a new theft to report, I will return. Perhaps you can speak to the sheriff since you are new to this —field work, I mean."

Belinda could feel herself blushing and hated it. "Thank you."

"And call me Lionel. The mayor is Calverson. If we're going to work together to prove Dwight innocent, I want to be on a first-name basis. Is that all right with you?"

"Most certainly," Belinda said. She pulled open the drawer to her immediate right and pulled out a contract form Adelaide had printed up. She slid it across the desk to him. "You may take this with you and review it. When you come back, we can discuss terms. I don't know how much work will need to be done. Please be assured that if I have any questions about how to proceed with field work, I'll consult with my sisters through correspondence."

"I'm sure you'll do whatever you need to do. Now, what information do you need from me at this time?"

5

———

When Lionel stepped into Dwight's office at Big T Ranch, he went directly to the window and pulled his pipe from his pocket. He clutched it between his teeth as he patted his breast pockets and lower pockets of his jacket. He reached into the inner pocket of his jacket and pulled out a packet of dried leaves, some of which he dumped into the bowl of the pipe. He twisted the top of the bag to close it and tucked it back where he got it from.

He lit the pipe with a match and took a few puffs without speaking.

Dwight was behind his desk, writing a letter. He seemed very concentrated on it, and Lionel didn't want to interrupt him. He waited until Dwight sat back before turning at his friend.

"Who's the letter to, if you don't mind me asking?"

"One of the women who has written to me about coming here to be my bride. You know I placed that ad a couple of weeks ago. I've got some letters here. Just writing back."

"So you're really going through with that?" Lionel asked. "Not that I have anything against it. I just thought you would find a woman here in Sacramento."

Dwight sighed heavily. "Nah. I've been trying, and it seems to me that too many ladies are listening to the rumors rather than listening to me."

Lionel sucked his teeth. "This a big city. Surely there's someone."

Dwight dropped the pen on the desk and gave his friend a narrow look. "I've tried, Lionel. I'm done trying. I've had it with the women here. I want a woman who is willing to get to know me before they hear about what an awful son I was."

"You weren't an awful son," Lionel remarked, moving from the window to the chair on the opposite side of Dwight's desk.

He snorted. "I know that. You know that. Them.

Out there. They don't know that. Or they do and just need someone to be angry with. They act like I came back and murdered Pa myself. Tired of it. I didn't even have time to grieve before they were harassing me for not coming back sooner."

"You couldn't," Lionel responded in a tense voice.

Dwight gave him a direct look. "As I said, I know that, and so do you."

Lionel shook his head, feeling sorry for his best friend. "You're right. I'm sorry. I understand the logic behind what you're doing."

Dwight sat back abruptly, making the cushion on the back of his chair hiss when he pressed on it. "It's been five years. They're never going to listen to me. Five years is long enough for them to change their minds. But they aren't going to. Never. And I'm tired of waiting and looking. I'm thirty years old. I need to get married. You might not be interested in marriage, but I am. I want a son. An heir. If not a son, a beautiful daughter, who will find a good man, and I can leave her and her husband my ranch."

"Maybe by then, you'll be able to just leave it to your daughter. The women are making big strides in that area, you know." Lionel shifted in the seat, taking a few puffs from his pipe. The smell of the sweet herbs filled the room. "So tell me. What if you're charged with this cattle rustling, and you have a bride here? What will she do then? You'll have to trust her enough to marry her quickly."

Dwight chuckled, which made Lionel feel a little better inside. He was glad to bring at least a small smile to his friend's face. "You'll just have to take my place. You aren't married. You can take her as your bride, and you two can live happily together on my ranch."

Lionel shook his head, knowing his friend was joking. "Not gonna happen. First off, you won't be charged with the crime. Second, I would never take the woman you've chosen to marry. We don't have the same taste in women. We've always known that. That's why we got along so well through the years."

Dwight let out a brief chuckle. "Maybe that's one of the reasons. And I'm glad you think I won't get charged. Right now, things aren't looking so good."

"I don't want you to worry about it," Lionel remarked. "I have someone working on it. You'll be able to sleep well soon."

Lionel watched his friend's face, where a soft look of interest appeared, much to Lionel's relief.

The few occasions that cattle had been stolen, Dwight had been on his own, no one to vouch for his whereabouts. The handkerchief had been found, and he was sure that wasn't the last item that would be left to prove Dwight was somehow responsible. In addition to that, Big T was doing exceptionally well after the mild winter they'd had, which only made the sheriff and would surely make the inspector think that extra money was coming from the stolen cattle when Dwight auctioned it off.

He knew in his heart that Dwight was innocent of the charges. But he did admit it didn't look good, either.

"And what exactly do you mean by that?"

Lionel had to think quickly. He'd thought that it would be best for Belinda to come to the ranch undercover. "I, uh, can't say who it is. This person is working, shall we say, behind the scenes? It's necessary for you not to know what's going on so the law can't say you paid someone to fabricate evidence."

Dwight nodded. "Someone is doing a good job making it look like I'm behind the cattle rustling. You're right. I don't want to know. But what if this man wants to interview me?"

Lionel bit back a snicker. "Don't worry," he said firmly. "He won't."

He stood up again and went to the window, looking out over the land that stretched out to the right of the gigantic three-story ranch house. He let himself grin. It was a funny thought that he didn't technically lie to Dwight. Belinda Salinger was far from being a man. She was all woman.

Lionel had noticed the moment he went into the agency how refreshing Belinda was to him. She had dark locks and the most intense hazel eyes he'd ever seen. The first thing he noticed was that her eyes were naturally narrow, only showing a small portion of her actual eyeballs. Her lashes were long, and he'd thought several times that she was fluttering them at him but quickly realized that it was just her blinking.

He liked her right away. She was honest. She didn't have to admit to him that she'd done no field work before. That was actually a plus if she came to do undercover work, in his opinion. She was obviously no dunce. She wouldn't slip up and say why she was there. She would be more natural with Dwight. It would be easier to get the information she needed.

"You'll want to deny accountability to the law, Dwight," Lionel said. "Better you don't know anything at all about this person."

"If you say so, Lionel," Dwight said. Lionel glanced back at him. He'd picked up his pen and was tapping it against his lip, his eyes on the paper in front of him. "I trust you. I've always trusted you to do the right thing for me. You give me good advice. Always have."

Lionel gave his friend a smile through the pipe clutched between his teeth. "You're my best friend, Dwight. I'm not gonna do you wrong."

6

Sheriff John Nolan was in charge of the County of Josephson, which was where Big T Ranch was located. Belinda made an arrangement to meet with him and arrived on time, keeping her nervous anxiety to herself. She had no idea if the man would even talk to her. Having done no field work, she didn't know how receptive people were to answering questions posed by a woman—especially men in law enforcement.

She went in without knocking and walked directly to the office to the left with the word SHERIFF painted on the glass of the upper half. She knocked and went in when she heard a man say, "Come in."

He stood up and gave her a pleasant smile. She

was glad to see it. She moved forward, holding her hand out. "Hello. I'm Belinda Salinger from the Wagon Wheel Justice Agency."

"Gabriel's agency," the man exclaimed to her surprise.

She lifted her eyebrows. "Yes. That's right."

He pumped her hand enthusiastically. "I knew Gabe very well. He was a good friend of mine. Helped me with several cases. You must be his niece, is that right?"

"That's correct, sir. He was my uncle. He passed a few years ago."

"I remember. I was at the funeral. I think I saw you there. With your sisters. You have four, is that right?"

Belinda settled in the chair across from him while he sat in his. "I have three sisters. There are four of us total."

"Ah. Well, I must say, he spoke so highly of the four of you. I knew he was going to leave his agency to you girls. He said you were all brilliant and had picked up the craft quickly and easily."

Belinda was surprised to hear her uncle had been talking about them so frequently. Sheriff Nolan had no jurisdiction in the County of Sacramento, where the agency was. That meant her uncle had spoken about them no matter where he was. She felt a pang of nostalgia and pulled in a sharp breath.

"That's nice to hear," she said, somewhat breathlessly. "It hasn't been even two years since we lost him, and it still feels like yesterday."

The sheriff pulled his eyebrows together and gave her a sympathetic look. "Let's not talk about that anymore, then. I can see it's upsetting you. What can I do to help you here today? You haven't come just to have a chat, have you? Not that I mind."

"I am on a case," Belinda said, feeling much more confident than when she'd come in. "I know you will be able to help me, as this is taking place in your jurisdiction."

Sheriff Nolan lifted his eyebrows. "You must be talking about the cattle rustling."

Belinda couldn't help reacting with surprise. "Is that the only crime going on right now in this whole county?"

Sheriff Nolan chuckled. "I sure hope so. It's the biggest case we have, and I don't think you would have gotten involved if it was anything smaller. I have to say we have a suspect in the case. You will want to speak to him." His face changed, and he narrowed his eyes. "Unless he's the one who hired you."

"Are you speaking of Dwight Barnes?" Belinda asked. She wasn't going to tell Sheriff Nolan who had hired her. It was best to be kept anonymous.

"That's right. He the one who hired you?"

Belinda shook her head. "I won't reveal who hired me, but I will tell you it wasn't Dwight Barnes. I was told he was the suspect you're looking at right now, and my goal is to prove what is true and what is not true. If Dwight is behind the cattle rustling, I will find out. If he is innocent, despite the way many seem to feel about him in this county, I will find out. And I will not hesitate to tell the truth and make sure the criminals are brought to justice."

The sheriff sat back, contemplating her for a moment. "I believe you. Tell me, how did you come across the case if Dwight didn't hire you?"

"I read about it in the paper." To prove she wasn't lying, Belinda abruptly held up a folded paper she'd had tucked next to her on the chair. She had picked up a paper that very morning and searched for an article about the cattle rustling.

The sheriff's eyes averted to the paper and then back to her.

"I'd like to find out as much as I can about this Dwight character." She used the term to make herself more hospitable to the sheriff, who seemed to have an opinion of Dwight himself, and it wasn't a good one. "What can you tell me about him?"

"I can tell you he's not trustworthy," the sheriff began. "Some five years ago or so, his father fell ill. He survived six months, waiting, hoping for his son to return home and be with him on his deathbed. Did Dwight return? No, he didn't. He didn't show up until the day of the funeral. He made some excuse about not being able to come back before, but we all know he was just waiting for Tom to die so he could take over the ranch."

"Were he and his father on bad terms when he originally left home? Where did Dwight go?"

The sheriff seemed to think about it a moment before answering, "I don't remember them being on bad terms. In fact, Dwight was always as beloved as his father here in Josephson County. But when he didn't come back, when he showed no respect for his father, we all knew what he'd become. He went off to get educated, had his adventures, and was too busy to come back when his father needed him."

Belinda thought for a moment. "What was his reason? The one he gave to you all when he came back?"

The sheriff was quiet, shuffling in his seat. "I

don't even remember now," he grumbled. "Something unacceptable. Unbelievable."

Belinda felt a sudden anxiousness to meet the man they were talking about. Lionel had talked about him in such glowing terms. He'd stayed an extra hour giving her information about Dwight. Now, to hear the sheriff give her the exact opposite opinion seemed strange.

"I'll have to interview him," she said, thinking aloud.

"Yes, that would be wise," he responded. "I'm not sure how much I would believe, though. He's a liar through and through."

"I thought you said he was well-loved before he left town," Belinda said in a curious voice.

The man nodded. "He was."

"How could it have gone so far in the other direction? It seems like you hate him."

The sheriff pursed his lips and drew in a deep breath through his nose, making his large chest bulge out. He let the breath out and said in a deep voice, "It was the disappointment. That he couldn't bring himself to get back here for Tom. We don't hate him. We are so deeply disappointed in him, it seems unforgivable that he didn't do the right thing."

Belinda absorbed the information. "I think I

might have to go in undercover," she said. "I will have to pose as someone else—perhaps a member of the staff—and I will need you to give me some leeway if I do that. It means I will be around him more, and I need you not to give me away."

The sheriff nodded. "Anything for the niece of Gabe Salinger. I trusted him. I will trust you."

"Thank you."

When the sheriff spoke again, his voice had changed. Now Belinda could hear how upset the whole thing made him.

"He was such an upstanding young man. Friends with Lionel Calverson, our local hero. Treating everyone with respect. Never getting in trouble with the law. Never getting in trouble with anyone." He shook his head. "An upstanding young man. Too bad he had to change the way he did."

7

Lionel propped up the barn door while Dwight hammered a board in place.

"You should really be getting your ranch hands to do this, Dwight," Lionel remarked.

Dwight glanced at him over his shoulder, sweat beading on his forehead. "You volunteered to help with this, buddy. Quit complaining."

Lionel grunted. "Yeah, yeah." He begrudgingly held the door up a few minutes longer while Dwight screwed it to the jamb. He had, in fact, offered his assistance and didn't mind helping with the labor work in the least. To him, it didn't matter how much money he had in the bank. It wasn't money he'd earned himself. It was given to him by his father for working in the office of the mayor and, before that, the law office his father had owned. He'd sold the law firm to his protégé when Lionel made it perfectly clear he was not only not going to be a lawyer, but he also wasn't vying for any position in politics either.

"All done. I guess you need a break now, weepy?"

Lionel let out an abrupt laugh. "Weepy? That's a new one." He couldn't help laughing hard and was glad when Dwight joined him. They didn't get to laugh much anymore. The case was weighing heavily on Dwight, and Lionel didn't know what to do other than to be by his side and try to make him laugh. And hire a female private investigator. A very pretty private investigator.

Their laughter died when they turned from the barn and saw a pair of horses headed their way. Lionel immediately recognized the horse of the sheriff and then the man on top. Next to him was Inspector Binks, looking a bit too triumphant for Lionel's tastes. He quickly thought of which lawyer he would hire to defend his best friend.

He sighed heavily and turned to the side, so he was facing Dwight, but his eyes were on the sky as he silently asked God why this was happening. He slapped the gloves he'd just taken off into one hand.

Dwight groaned, not taking his eyes from the men. He stayed where he was, crossing his arms in front of his chest. His stance was automatically defensive.

"Gentlemen," he said in a polite tone, though his face was saying something completely opposite. Lionel didn't even look at the men.

"We have some new questions for you, Dwight," the sheriff said coolly. "Maybe you'd like to come with us inside, and we can talk?"

"I don't want you in my house," Dwight replied, his voice equally icy. "You might plant something in there to incriminate me and say that it proves I'm guilty. Which I'm not. I have nothing to do with the cattle rustling, and my friend here was right last time. This is harassment, and it needs to stop."

"We are investigating an ongoing crime, Mr. Barnes," Inspector Binks retorted. "Until the criminals are caught, we will ask whatever questions to whomever we please. We are aiming to get the truth."

"Who else have you been talking to every single day then?" Dwight asked angrily. "Who else do you harass the way you do me?"

"We have our suspects," the sheriff answered. "You just happen to be at the top of the list."

Dwight grumbled something impolite under his breath, turning away from the men.

"You may not realize that another theft was committed last night," Inspector Binks barked, his mustache twitching in a way that made Lionel want to laugh. "Just come clean, Mr. Barnes. Confess so this can be over with."

"What?" Lionel's ire shot up from his spine, making his head feel hot. He stepped in front of Dwight, glaring at the lawman. "You're telling him to confess because you believe he's guilty. That's not right. That's not justice. He isn't guilty, and you have to prove him guilty before you hang him."

"Our goal is not to hang him," the inspector remarked, humor in his voice, "unless, of course, he commits a murder. Have you committed murder as well as cattle theft, Mr. Barnes?"

Lionel took another step forward so that he was within a foot of the horse the man was riding. "You will need to come back another time, Inspector. Dwight and I have a lot of work to do. I'll be speaking to my father about this behavior. As mayor, he has the right to oversee how this investigation is going. I'm sure a word from me will have him on your back faster than you can say blink."

Lionel was uncomfortable with throwing his father in the inspector's face, especially since the mayor was probably on the side of the lawmen. He'd expressed for the last five years how upset he was that Lionel was still Dwight's best friend, after Dwight's inability to return until after his father passed. He was constantly complaining about something Dwight was doing in town, if he participated on any committees or tried to make improvements to Sacramento in one way or another. He'd even object to Dwight's plan to carve out a road leading in a winding pattern to all of the ranches in Josephson County, making delivery and pick up of supplies much easier and faster for the residents of those ranches.

Fortunately, the road had been cut. It proved to be a great benefit to the surrounding ranches. They were grateful to Dwight for it and showed their appreciation by coming by randomly, talking to him about his father, and getting more information directly from him about what had happened to prevent him from returning.

Then the sabotage had started. That was one thing Dwight and Lionel noticed on Big T Ranch that was the same as the other ranches. They had been sabotaged, fences broken, holes dug deep for cattle to fall in and break their legs, even outbuildings set ablaze. Nothing had been done to stop those things from expanding into the theft.

"Your wagon was spotted last night," the sheriff said in a victorious voice.

Lionel sneered.

"Where the theft took place?" he asked, already knowing the answer.

"No."

Lionel's eyebrows shot up in surprise.

"It was seen going down the road in the middle of the night. The owners of the ranch that was struck —and I'm not going to tell you their names since you already know, and if you don't, I don't want you retaliating against them for telling us about you."

Dwight let out an exasperated breath, giving the sheriff a sarcastic look. "You don't really expect me to believe anyone saw my wagon, that they would absolutely know it was *my wagon* in the middle of the night, do you?"

The sheriff shrugged. "Said you had a couple of lanterns swingin' from the front, and they saw the markings on the side. Same as the handkerchief. Big T Ranch. BTR. You won't get away with this for much longer, son. Why don't you just confess?"

"You need to leave," Lionel said firmly. "Dwight is getting his lawyers, and they will contact you. If you have anything further to say, just go through them."

Lionel hoped he wasn't overstepping his bounds. He was just used to taking care of his friend and standing up for him. He'd done it since their very early years and couldn't seem to stop now, over twenty years later.

He glanced at Dwight to gauge his friend's reaction to what he was saying. Dwight's jaw was visibly clenched, and his arms were folded over his chest. He was glaring at the inspector with great hatred. He wished he could calm Dwight down so he wouldn't show so much anger toward the lawmen. But there was nothing he could say. Dwight was being harassed and mistreated.

Lionel wasn't about to tell his friend how to feel about that.

The inspector and the sheriff backed their horses up a few paces before turning them around. They said nothing more as they left Big T Ranch.

"You're right, Lionel," Dwight said, his voice deep and angry. "It's time I called Bruce. I should have as soon as this started. He'll know what to do." His face was red, and he stomped off toward the house.

Lionel came up behind him and kept pace. "Try not to worry, Dwight," he remarked, keeping his voice low. "We've got help. Just try not to worry."

8

———

Belinda was excited to have Lionel in her office once again. She hoped it didn't show as much as she felt.

When he came in, and before he sat down, he made sure to shake her hand and smile wide. "Good to see you again," he said in a warm voice.

"Likewise," she responded. And she meant it. He was looking very nice in a suit and tie, polished black shoes, and a tall black hat perched on his dark hair. His light brown eyes gazed at her from behind long brown lashes. He was a fine-looking man, that was for sure.

"So I've done some research into the case," she said, after clearing her throat and brushing her hands under her to sit down without her skirt being poofed up under her. She dropped her eyes to the folder she'd started to help her keep track of the case in a more organized fashion. She flipped it open and picked up the paper on top. "I've made some notes. I'm going to take the case, by the way, and if you want to go over our standard contract and sign it, that would be perfect."

Lionel nodded, pulling a folded paper from the inside breast pocket of his jacket. He handed it to her. "I've taken the liberty of filling it out with my offer. If it isn't enough, we can certainly adjust it. I've already signed it. All it needs is your signature."

Belinda raised her eyebrows. She took the paper from him and unfolded it. She stared down at the number he'd written, a chill spreading over her. She'd never been offered that much money before.

"I... I don't know if it would be ethical to take this much. We are not poor, Mr. Cal... Lionel. We aren't about to close our doors."

He laughed. "If you want me to pay you less, I will." He held out his hand for the paper.

She grinned, sticking out the tip of her tongue and pressing the paper against her chest. "Maybe it *is* ethical," she remarked, making him laugh again.

"All right." He chuckled as he said the word. "So that's taken care of. But I have a suggestion, and I think you'll understand why I offered you so much money when you hear it."

Belinda was a little uneasy hearing that. She was still willing to listen, however. She was sure Lionel wouldn't propose anything that would be harmful to her.

"I'll listen, but I want you to know where I'm coming from as well. I need to talk to the ranch hands at Big T, and I need to talk to Dwight."

"You'll want to talk to the foreman. His name is Mick. He's a character. Not a real good character. I hate to put my opinion in, but there's something off about that man. You'll definitely want to talk to him and give me your opinion."

"I was thinking about ways to get in there undercover. I would rather talk to Dwight and the others without them knowing why I'm there. I was thinking about being hired on as staff, but I don't feel comfortable taking money from him when I'm working and especially after this contract amount." She pushed the paper toward him before sitting forward abruptly. "Oh, I suppose I should sign this, as well. We will need to make a second copy for your records."

Lionel chuckled. "All right. And getting hired on as staff is a good idea. Help are never noticed. You could overhear a lot of conversations. But I don't think you will be able to openly ask Dwight any questions. He wouldn't be obliged to answer them, would he? And how would you really get to know him if you're just the help? He won't pay any attention to you. All that you'd find would be hearsay. Not really helpful."

"Do you have a better idea?"

Lionel looked contemplative. "I might."

Belinda was intrigued. His expression was mischievous.

"What are you thinking?"

"I was talking to Dwight yesterday, and... well, I'll just be blunt. The man is lonely. He's had a hard time with the ladies in Sacramento because they all know someone who knew his pa, and when he didn't, well, there's a..."

Belinda decided to spare him the uncomfortableness of telling on his friend. "The sheriff filled me in on the opinion of many in this city. He didn't come back before his father died. Everyone is angry because they think he should have made the time. I'll tell you, I was taken aback by the way the sheriff spoke about him. It was completely the opposite of your opinion of him. I need to get a really good representation of who he really is, and I can't fathom a way to really do that. Why would I make friends with him? Why would he want to trust me at all?"

"I'm glad you know about the situation. Maybe you'll understand why Dwight decided to seek a mail-order bride from one of the magazines."

Belinda's eyebrows shot up in the air. "Really? How interesting."

"I saw three letters from ladies who responded to his ad."

"Wait a minute," Belinda said, sitting forward and putting up one finger to stop him. "Are you suggesting what I believe you are suggesting?"

"I think I might be," Lionel said in a conspiratorial way, grinning at her.

"No," she replied, sitting back, blinking at him. "You don't really want me to pose as one of those ladies, do you?"

"Can you think of a better way to get in there and really get to know him?"

Belinda thought about it for a moment. It seemed incomprehensible. How could she pose as a woman she didn't even know?

"I wouldn't know what the woman has written to him. I wouldn't know anything about her. How would we make this work?"

"I've been thinking about it. Here." He pulled a

second paper from his pocket and handed it to him. It turned out to be a folded envelope with a letter inside. He pointed at the envelope. "It's from Marie B. Wright. You could say the B stands for Belinda , and that's what you like to be called. That way, you'll be responding to your actual name. I took the liberty of reading the letter, and it's all basic and common. A sister and father in San Diego. No real prospects or interests in life. Just a nice sounding woman. I don't know if that's the one I saw him writing a letter to, but if I know Dwight, he wrote a letter to all three."

Belinda swallowed, her hands slightly shaking as she pulled the paper from the envelope. "I don't know if I can pull this off," she whispered softly. "I have a feeling I'm going to have to, though."

She quickly read through the letter and agreed with Lionel that Marie seemed quite common and plain. She didn't describe herself, so Belinda could pass as the woman.

"What if... what do I do, just show up and say, Hello, I wrote to you, and here I am without being invited?"

"Why not? Maybe she's desperate. He wouldn't know, would he?"

"Wouldn't he tell me to go on back home?"

"No." Lionel sounded confident, shaking his head. "That's not the Dwight I know. He will give you a chance just because you came all the way from..." He lifted out of his seat and leaned forward, his eyes on the envelope on the desk, "San Diego. San Diego? I thought they were all east coast. You have a bit of an east coast accent."

"I'll do fine. But what if he wants to get intimate with me? I can't do anything like that."

Lionel let out a loud laugh. "Dwight? Not a chance, dear lady. He is a gentleman. You can tell him you want a spare room and that you are not going to do anything with him until after you're married. You will never marry him, so you won't have to worry about that. And I'm sure you will be nice to him. It's not like you will be cruel to him."

"No. I would never."

"Then what do you say? Are you ready for an adventure?"

She grinned at him. His enthusiasm was contagious. "Definitely ready for an adventure."

9

———

The next day, Belinda walked around the business district of Sacramento, enjoying the shops, purchasing new clothes to use for her undercover job. She didn't want to wear her own clothes when she was pretending to be someone else.

She imagined Marie to be quite a plain woman, wearing sensible clothes and shoes and not going with any of the latest styles. She wouldn't make the woman unattractive, but she didn't want to be flashy and try to get Dwight's attention in that way either. Her plan was to get the information she needed to clear his name, come clean, and get on back home. She hoped it wouldn't take longer than a week, but she was prepared to stay for longer. Her sisters wouldn't be back for at least a month, though Sadie and Larson would be returning in three, depending on the outcome of the case they were on.

She thought about the arrangements she had made as she walked, taking in the dresses, hats, gloves, furniture, so many beautiful things displayed behind the glass in the front of the shops. She had the money to buy whatever she wanted, but Belinda was a frugal woman and wasn't about to spend a lot of money on herself.

She passed the mayor's office and glanced in the window. She was shocked to see Lionel in the front office, easily seen through the large wall-to-wall window. She wouldn't have been surprised to see him if he wasn't at that moment arguing with the mayor, his father, Jack Calverson.

Her curiosity was strong. She hadn't done enough work in the field, she decided, because she was so interested in what they were talking about, she backed up and turned her back to the window. She looked around, but no one was paying any attention to her. She was used to that and was now grateful to have a reason not to be upset about it.

The door to the mayor's office was closed. She looked around again before backing up to it and putting one hand behind her back, wrapping her fingers around the long vertical handle. She turned it lightly, praying it wouldn't click loudly. It didn't, and she breathed a sigh of relief when she felt a rush of air brush against her arm. She dropped her arm after pushing the door just an inch open. It was enough to let the sound of the men's voices come through loud and clear. She stayed where she was, blocking the door, hoping no one would notice her, and the men inside wouldn't notice the door cracked open.

"I am done with this behavior, Lionel," the mayor was saying or more literally growling. "You are bringing shame on our name. Is that what you want for our family? Do you want to shame our family?"

"Supporting my friend, whom I believe to be innocent, is not bringing shame to our name, Father. You only say that because you move in circles that echo your opinion. Not everyone holds Dwight's reasoning against him. We believe in him. We know he's innocent. Big T has suffered from sabotage just like the other ranches."

"Likely done by his own hand."

"That's utterly ridiculous, Father, and you know it," Lionel roared, making Belinda jump and widen her eyes. "He is completely innocent, and we are going to prove it."

"Who is we?" his father asked. "There is no one but you. Even the ranch hands working on the Big T ranch believe their boss to be guilty."

"No, they don't," Lionel retorted. "They are split. And you know how they are split? The ones who've been listening to your tripe believe him to be guilty. Those of us who work and spend time with him day after day know that he's innocent."

"You must come to accept that your friend is not a trustworthy man. You cannot count on him. If his own father couldn't count on him, what makes you think you can?"

"I don't want to hear that," Lionel snapped. Belinda heard him moving around the room. He slammed something on a table or desktop. "You know full well why he wasn't here. You don't want to believe him. I will never understand why you and others in this city decided to feel this way about Dwight. He's an innocent man, and I'm going to prove it. I have help. Expert help. We're going to prove him innocent."

"You might want to think twice about that, Lionel," Jack responded, his voice so ice-cold, it gave Belinda chills. "If you do not want to be cut off from the family fund, you will stop this pointless pursuit and let Inspector Binks and Sheriff Nolan do their jobs."

"That inspector is a joke," Lionel spat out. "And Sheriff Nolan has his own personal reasons for acting the way he's acting. He's determined to put Dwight off Big T Ranch. He wants him in jail."

"I've made myself perfectly clear with you, son. I don't need to tell you this again. In fact, I won't tell you again. Stop interfering, or you will be cut off from the fund. I know that's not what you want."

Lionel didn't say anything for a moment, and Belinda's heart suddenly went into overdrive. Was he coming toward the door? He would notice it was cracked. Would he be angry that she was eavesdropping on his private conversation? Would he be forgiving because it was a conversation about Dwight?

Whether he was or not wasn't the real relevant question, though. The relevant question was, what would the mayor do when he saw her there? She might end up in jail herself.

She put her hand on the door handle, ready to pull it closed.

She hesitated, though, and heard Lionel's voice very low. She pictured him directly in front of his father, speaking directly into his face. "You have no power over me, Father. I am not one of your constituents. I didn't even vote for you in the last election. I don't care about your money. I have my own. I'm twenty-nine years old. You don't think I've made my own fortune myself?"

"Anything you've made, you've made because I gave you money in the beginning. Therefore all the money you have is actually mine."

Lionel let out an abrupt laugh. "No, Father. That's not going to work on me. I'm not stupid like your club friends. Don't try to take my money from me. You won't succeed. I'm not afraid of you. I never will be."

She heard a soft, subtle sound and hurriedly pulled the door closed, though she latched it as quietly as she could. She hurried away from the door, going in the opposite direction from where she was originally going. Her heart pounded nervously, and she hid around the side of the building in the alley, placing one hand on her chest. She could hear her pulse beating in her ears.

She gulped and tried to breathe normally, closing her eyes.

"Belinda ?"

The sound of Lionel's voice saying her name

made her eyes open wide. She gasped and laughed softly. "Oh. I didn't see you there." She continued to laugh nervously.

He came into the alley and stood near her, giving her a strange look. She wondered if he knew she'd heard his argument with his father.

"You look flushed. Are you all right? Do you feel ill?"

"No, I... I'm fine." She tried hard to regain control. "I just... I don't know. It's a bit warm for me."

Lionel's eyebrows shot up. "Too warm?"

"A little?" She smiled at him.

"You're a strange woman, Belinda. Very strange, indeed."

10

————

Lionel's conversation with Belinda in the alley was brief. Lionel wasn't in the mood to talk to anyone. He was headed for Big T because it had the best trails, and he wanted to go for a long ride to clear his head. As much as he was beginning to enjoy Belinda's company and she was on his mind a bit more than she should be, all he wanted to do was be by himself.

He didn't ask permission to go on Big T for a ride, but he didn't have to. He and Dwight had been riding those trails since they were very young. There was one, in particular, they enjoyed the most, and that was the one he chose.

His aggravation with his father dominated his

thoughts as he rode along. He wasn't able to enjoy the trees, the gentle rustling of the leaves, the birds singing above his head, or even the bright blue sky and the sun with all its warmth.

The mayor was refusing to follow up on different paths of inquiry. His reasoning, in his opinion, was simple. Dwight was guilty.

Nothing irritated Lionel more than a man who was not willing to see more than one side of the story. Investigators and lawmen should be required to leave their personal opinions at the door. They should be neutral at all times. They were so certain Dwight was guilty, they weren't even trying to look anywhere else.

It was so obvious that someone was planting evidence against Dwight. He didn't understand how any logical person would not see that. Dwight wasn't stupid. He wasn't going to leave things behind. He wasn't going to let himself be seen in his wagon on the night of a theft.

He wasn't a criminal.

A crack of a twig ahead of him got his attention, and he stopped his horse. After a moment, he spotted a horse and rider coming up the trail around the gentle curve. It took about half a second before he saw that it was Dwight. His tension released a bit, and he moved his horse to continue toward his friend.

Dwight saw him and lifted a hand in the air as a greeting.

"Howdy," Lionel called out, hoping he and Dwight could find something amusing to laugh about. That seemed to be an unspoken pact between the men. When things were going wrong, one or the other would find a bit of humor hidden in the turmoil.

It had been Dwight that kept him going after the tragedy that almost took so many young lives on the semi-frozen lake when he was young. Unbeknownst to the rest of the community, who thought of Lionel as the hero they insisted he was, he had gone through a period of listlessness and unhappiness that didn't seem to have any reason for being there.

"Howdy," Dwight replied when he was a bit closer. "What are you doing out here?"

"I could ask you the same thing, and I bet we'd have the same answers."

"Thinking about my future," Dwight grumbled, pulling up next to Lionel. They let the horses shuffle about as they talked.

"Yeah, I guess that's about right," Lionel replied. "I'm thinking about the future, too. Except it's more like the present and what could happen now to affect the future. You never know what's gonna happen next. Had an argument with my Pa. I'm telling you, Dwight, he's an unreasonable man. It's hard to believe he can charm his way into getting so many people to vote for him."

"He's not gonna check behind the sheriff and this new inspector. I didn't even think he knew Inspector Binks."

"I don't know if he knew him before," Lionel replied, "but he's got him in his pocket now if he didn't before, I'll bet on that."

Dwight sighed heavily. Lionel didn't see any laughter in their near future. The accusations were weighing heavy on his friend. He hated to see it. He wanted to think of something funny to say, but he just wasn't in the mood."

"Come back to the ranch with me," Dwight said. "Let's get a drink and relax. I don't want to think about any of this anymore."

"You're going to anyway. How about a game of cards?"

"Sounds good."

Neither man spoke as they rode back along the

trail. This time, Lionel was able to hear the birds singing and notice the gentle smells of the woods around him. His friend's presence eased his temper enough to satisfy him. His chest had been tense and tight until he saw Dwight coming his way.

THEY WERE SETTLED IN, taking opposite sides of the card table, bourbon in glasses to the side, the bottle ready to pour more. Lionel's head was already spinning from the first few sips. It would calm his heart and mind, though, and the distraction of the card game would be good for them both.

Belinda was still on his mind. He wondered what she was doing outside his father's office earlier that day. She'd looked like someone had frightened her half to death. The thought that someone might have threatened her or chased her into that alley made Lionel's blood boil. But she hadn't admitted to that, and he could do nothing if he didn't know the facts.

It was ironic that he'd seen her right after his argument with his father. If anything, it was wonderful to know that just seeing her face helped him calm down at least a little. He wished he'd been able to talk to her about what had happened, but he was afraid she would think less of him since he was bucking up against his father, the mayor of their city. The ladies hadn't voted for his father. They hadn't yet come to Sacramento when the voting was held.

He also thought it was insane that he couldn't talk to Belinda about his father and couldn't talk to Dwight about Belinda. He wanted to so badly.

Belinda was expected to arrive the next day, sometime in the morning. She'd checked the train schedule and would be arriving after the 9:30 train from San Diego came into the station. That way, if Dwight checked, he would see the arrival of the train. Lionel didn't think Dwight would do much checking. He was an easy-going man.

Lionel was rather anxious to find out how Dwight was going to react to her coming to the ranch. He'd pictured several scenarios in his mind. It would be interesting to find out how it would go down.

The two men traded off winning through the six games they played, with it ending in a tie. When the hour grew late, Dwight told his friend to stay the night in one of the guest rooms. He'd had too much to drink, he said, and it wouldn't be prudent to ride his horse through the streets of Sacramento, barely able to hold onto the saddle. He was the mayor's son, after all.

This produced at least a bit of the laughter Lionel was hoping to generate. It wasn't much. But it was something.

11

———

Belinda trembled just slightly as she pulled herself up in the saddle of her horse. Her heart beat nervously, settling in for the ride to Big T Ranch. It was a half-hour ride to Josephson County where the ranch was, and she was hoping she would calm down before she got there.

It probably would have been more appropriate if she'd gotten a little experience with field work before she decided to go undercover. Lying didn't come naturally to her, and she was still reconciling herself with the fact that this was part of the job, and it couldn't really be considered lying if she had a good cause. It was work. Not complete and total deception.

Yet that seemed like such a lame excuse to her.

Still, she was hired to prove whether or not Dwight was innocent, and the only way she could gain his trust was to go through this charade.

Even thinking those words made Belinda feel bad. She was gaining his trust under false pretenses. Another thing that worried her was what she would do if her ruse sparked feelings on either side. What would happen if she fell in love with him and he discovered her lie? Or vice versa. If he fell in love with her, only to discover she wasn't who she said she was?

Things could get very complicated. People might get hurt.

Still, by the time she got to the edge of the property some twenty-five minutes later, she was determined to go through with it. She wasn't going to shirk her duties. Lionel was his best friend, and he'd condoned this plan. He'd helped think it up. It wasn't being done to hurt Dwight. That was the most important thing.

The outskirts of the Big T Ranch were some of the most beautiful lands Belinda had ever seen. Rolling hills of green, patches of trees, ponds surrounded by bushes and flowers, sculptures randomly placed so that they dotted the land and passersby could be amazed by their beauty from the road. She was amazed by how long the drive was to get to the actual house.

She got closer and gazed up at the three-story house looming over her. To her left, some thirty yards away, was a long narrow building with four windows in a row to the right of a door. That was the bunkhouse. There was another building behind it that she only saw a corner of and assumed that was where the ranch hands had their meals.

In the distance, past those two buildings, she saw a great barn stretching up into the sky. There were men all around it, but she spotted one in particular and knew it was Lionel from where she was. She moved her horse in the direction of the men and slowly made her way around the buildings. She came up through the trees and stopped while still hidden. The men were talking.

She assumed the man closest to Lionel was Dwight. He was a handsome man, at least six feet if not taller, with wavy blond hair. She couldn't see the color of his eyes from where she was, but they were light, either blue or green. Probably blue. He had broad shoulders and moved with the fluidity of a dancer. She was impressed immediately. She didn't see how he could possibly feel the need to seek a bride through ads. Surely women were flocking to him.

Dwight and Lionel moved away from the barn and stood to the side, looking at it. Where they stopped was closer to Belinda , and she could clearly hear their conversation.

"Mick said the bullpen fence was broken through again. But this time, it was Chance's and you know that animal didn't go anywhere." It was Lionel who spoke first. She wondered if he'd seen her in the woods behind them.

"I've had it with this," Dwight growled. Belinda was surprised to hear such a harsh tone come from him. He didn't look upset. His face was neutral, still as handsome as she'd thought right away. "I feel so helpless. The next thing to happen will be a fire, and someone will die, and they'll blame me and said I sabotaged my land, set fire to my own property, and hold me responsible for the death."

"That's not going to happen," Lionel said firmly. "You've got to stop thinking so negatively. Things are going to work themselves out. We just have to be vigilant. I'm gonna help you repair everything they break until they're caught."

The men were quiet for a moment, and Belinda

almost moved to introduce herself when Dwight spoke again.

"What I don't understand is why no one hears any of this happening. Mick isn't the only one who stays in the bunkhouse. Some of this property damage is happening right near them."

Lionel shrugged, shaking his head. "I've already told you how I feel about Mick. I don't think you should discount him as someone to be looking at."

"He's been my foreman since I got here and was before I got here. I can't doubt his loyalty."

"You can. And you should. When something like this is going on, you have to protect yourself. You have to question everyone. You can't trust anyone."

Dwight turned his head and looked at his friend. "So I can't trust you, then?"

Belinda watched Lionel's grin grow big when he looked back at Dwight. "I'm the exception in this case. You won't find anyone more dedicated to clearing your name than me."

"I know, Lionel. Thanks. I appreciate it."

"I'd never think you were sabotaging your own land anyway," Lionel continued. "I trust you. I know you."

"They know me, too. They just choose to think this way about me. It doesn't make it easier that none of my cattle are missing. It makes me look even more guilty."

"I know I keep asking you this but are you sure you don't know who could be doing this to you? Anyone that's been particularly hard on you since you came back?"

Belinda turned her eyes to Dwight's face, of which she could only see one side. She could see it had turned red and he didn't look at his friend. His arms were crossed over his chest. His fingers were gripping his arms so tightly she could see the indentions in his skin.

"No," he answered after a moment. "I've been thinking about it, I really have. But the general consensus is that I'm a heartless dirty dog for not coming back and that I don't deserve what my father left me."

Belinda had heard this before. She was already being deceptive. This was the second time she'd chosen to eavesdrop. She was still telling herself this was all part of the job, but she couldn't help feeling like she was out of her element. If she didn't relax into the job by the end of this case, she might consider a complete job change unless her sisters would let her stay in the office and out of the field.

The way it felt, she was thinking she might be

left as the only one who would still be working at all. It wasn't true, and she knew it. Sadie and Larson would at least be back to work when they finished their case.

She urged her horse further through to come out in the open. She pretended not to know the men were standing to her left. She kept her eyes on the men in the distance, working beyond the barn. Through her peripheral vision, she noticed Lionel's body jerk.

"Miss? Miss?" She heard Dwight saying.

Her eyes darted in Dwight's direction, and she stopped the horse, putting on a warm smile.

"Hello," she said in her most formal voice. "I'm looking for Dwight Barnes?"

"You've found him," Dwight said pleasantly, coming toward her.

Lionel came close behind him, his eyes wide as he looked up at her. Dwight held his hand up to her, and she leaned to shake it.

"I'm Belinda Wright. Formally Marie, but I go by Belinda. I wrote an answer to your ad. I hope you don't mind my intrusion. I found myself in a position where I was forced to go somewhere, and so here I am. Uninvited. I apologize."

She was amazed by the mix of emotions that ran

through his features. He blinked rapidly, looking stunned at first. Then confused. The confusion stayed prominent as he struggled to quickly come to terms with what was happening.

Belinda realized she was holding her breath and tried to let it out slowly so it couldn't be heard. All she wanted was for him to say something.

"Oh," he finally said. "I... uh..."

"This is quite a surprise, isn't it?" Lionel said, coming forward. "Why don't you two go in the house and get better acquainted?"

"You have a lovely home here," Belinda said, prolonging their conversation. She didn't want to be inside alone with Dwight. She was more at ease with Lionel around. "This land... it's so peaceful and lovely. I must say I didn't expect to come to Sacramento and find this. In San Diego, it is very much a city."

"Sacramento is like that in the business district," Dwight replied cordially. He held up his hand. "Come down, and we'll take your horse to the stables. I'm sure we can find a stall for him."

Belinda grinned, relief flooding her. "Thank you so much."

12

———

Lionel shouldn't have been surprised to see her, but he was. She'd said she was coming. But when she'd emerged from the woods, riding casually on the back of that horse, Lionel had almost given himself away with his reaction.

He'd used the jerking motion to prompt getting Dwight's attention like he hadn't seen the woman ride onto his property.

If the situation had been normal, he would have offered to take her horse to the stable so Dwight and Belinda could walk and talk. But he didn't want to. It was strange. He felt almost protective of her. What if she slipped and said something to make Dwight suspicious?

"So you said something happened," Dwight said as they walked slowly toward the stables, "do you mind telling me anything about it? I hate to think you were in such a bad position that you had to come here out of the blue. Not that I mind," he added quickly. "I just hate to hear about people in dire situations. Of course I will open my home to you. But I'd like a few more details if you don't mind."

"Of course," Belinda responded in a tense tone, but Lionel thought it sounded more nervous than anything else. He had no idea if she'd planned a story to explain her abrupt arrival, but when she began to talk, he couldn't help thinking she was a natural for the job. "I'm not sure how much I told you about my situation in my letter. So much has happened. I have forgotten much of what I wrote. I can simply expand on what I already told you if you remind me what it was."

Lionel was blown away by her brilliance. What better way to find out than to ask point-blank? He pressed his lips together and turned his head away from Dwight even though his friend wasn't looking at him.

"You didn't say much in your letter. Your brother has left home leaving you and your mother, who has been urging you to move out on your own. I didn't realize you were in dire need of assistance. Your letter made no mention of it."

"Oh, I see," Belinda nodded. "I neglected to mention that mama is... that is she was deathly ill. She..." Belinda hesitated, dropping her eyes to the ground. Lionel once again had to look away so as not to give away his admiration for her acting ability. "She is no longer with us. I found myself without my mother's help, and so I needed to leave San Diego as quickly as possible. I didn't want to live out my days there anyway, as you might have noticed by the letter I wrote to you."

"Oh, my," Dwight said, his voice filled with sympathy. "I'm so sorry for your loss. Please, let me offer you a warm room, a fire in the hearth, and food in your belly until you decide what you want to do. There is no need to insist on marriage with me if you feel that's not what you want after spending some time here."

Belinda looked surprised. Lionel could see that emotion was genuine. "I would say that I hate to impose, but I did come all this way without noti-fying you first. I should have sent a telegraph. I..." She blushed heavily. "I was afraid I would be turned away. I really had no other prospects at all. I didn't write to anyone else. I'm sorry. I really do apologize."

"Enough of that. We're moving on from that." Dwight turned Belinda to him, and Lionel watched as he gave her a warm, friendly look. "You are welcome here, all right? I'm not going to turn you away. Just let me know if you need anything from me. If there's anything I can do to make your stay easier."

Lionel listened to his friend ease Belinda's anxiety. He was impressed. Dwight knew what it was like to be lost and not have any support to rely on.

Lionel went into the stable, leaving Belinda and Dwight outside. He had a strange feeling in his chest, and he was in full-blown denial about what it was.

He didn't really care for seeing Dwight holding Belinda so closely. And they weren't even hugging. What would he do when they were that close together? And why was he even feeling that way to begin with? He was feeling possessive for no reason.

He left the horse with Andy, the groom, and headed back to the front of the stables, hurrying his steps. He wasn't going to be with the two for very much longer and had to make sure that before they were alone together, they were getting along well.

He stepped out into the bright sunlight to see they had started toward the house already. He watched them walking, halting his own steps.

He chewed on his bottom lip, leaving his eyes on the back of Belinda's head, wishing he was in Dwight's place at that moment and then wondering where these feelings were coming from.

He turned away from the two and walked toward the ranch hands working behind the barn. Before he got to them, he realized that he was going in the wrong direction. He didn't have to work. He was only there for Dwight. The ranch hands were paid for the work they were doing.

He abruptly turned on his heel and went straight back to the stables.

"Back again already? Need her horse?" Lionel lifted his chin once, realizing the groom had been watching what was going on.

"No," Lionel replied, "I need mine."

Andy looked a little surprised but stepped over to the stall where Lionel's horse was waiting. He released the latch and pulled the stall door toward him. The horse lifted his large head and nodded at Lionel.

"There you are, boy," he murmured, entering the stall to prepare the horse for a ride. He had been recently scrubbed and brushed apparently because his coat was shining and beautiful. "Thanks for taking care of her today, Andy. You didn't have to do that."

"Hope I didn't step on your toes, Mr. Calverson," the young man replied. "He wasn't excessively dirty. I just thought he might like a bath and a brushing. He's a real good horse. You lucked out on him."

"Definitely blessed, yes," Lionel responded. He went about setting his saddle on the animal's back and ensuring the straps weren't too tight around his large body.

He led the horse outside and pulled up into the saddle, gathering the reins in his hand. He urged Champion forward with a kick of his heels and directed the animal toward the main road. As he went down the long path, he looked from side to side, trying to picture it through new eyes, how Belinda must have seen it. It really was beautiful land. It had been a long time since he complimented his friend on the beauty of it.

He was already at his father's office when he started to regret ever leaving the ranch. It was the right thing to do. He knew that. But it still felt like he was remiss in leaving. He should have stayed. If only to make sure she didn't give away his part in the whole scheme. Not that he had any suspicion she would do that.

He was just trying to find excuses for why he should have stayed.

He hopped up the steps and went into the building. His father was in his office with the door open and looked up when his son came in.

"Lionel," he called out.

Lionel was in no mood to talk to his father.

"I'll talk to you later, Pa," he yelled over his shoulder. "Too busy right now."

13

———————

Belinda was impressed with the house the moment she walked in. She'd never seen so much space in all her life. She couldn't imagine living there as a single man. An older man dressed like a butler came from one of the other rooms. Belinda assumed he'd heard the front door and the sound of their feet on the hardwood floors beneath her feet. He stopped and stared at her, a stunned look on his face. It only lasted a moment before he recovered and approached, a look of curiosity on his face as he looked at his boss.

"Sir?" he said.

"Henry, this is Belinda. She will be our guest for a time. Belinda , this is Henry, my butler."

"Nice to meet you," Belinda said, putting out her

hand. He didn't take it but rather glanced down at it and then back up at her, bowing from the waist.

"Terribly nice to meet you, as well, Miss." He raised his eyebrows when saying the last word.

"Yes, she's a Miss," Dwight said. "I'm going to show her around the house and then to the guest room down the hall from my room. If you will please give it a quick dusting and make sure it has been aired out before we get up there, that would be appreciated."

"Yes, sir, I'll get to that right now."

He nodded and bowed before turning to the long set of stairs and quickly moving up them.

"A beautiful home to match the beautiful land around it," Belinda observed, somewhat breathlessly. She spun around in a slow circle, taking in the vast area of the foyer. Along the walls were elegant stands with decoratively colored vases holding flowers that matched the main color of the container they were in.

"Thank you. This is actually my father's home. He died five years ago after a short illness and left it all to me. I try to keep it as clean and lovely as it was when he was alive."

"Is your mother still with us?" Belinda asked softly, hoping it wasn't a touchy subject.

"No, she died when I was a baby," Dwight answered, offering her his elbow. "I have no memory of her. Would you like a tour?"

"I would love one, thank you."

Dwight took her from room to room, first the dining room to the left of the entrance, which was vast and decorated with black, yellow, and gold furniture. There were drapes and a swirling rug on the floor that was a definite eye-catcher.

The ranch was home to a library with many books Belinda wished she would have time to read, a game room with a billiards table and many other tables for cards, a sunroom that took up the entire back of the house and his office, which was connected and had glass on two sides, as it was in the back right corner of the structure.

The parlor and den were the other two rooms on the right side of the house from the entrance. The den was decorated with deep reds and dark browns. She couldn't believe the comfortable atmosphere she felt when she stepped in. She hoped to spend much of her time in that room. It was the exact opposite of the sunroom, dark, brooding, the perfect atmosphere for a blazing fire during the winter, a blanket over the legs and a good book read by the light of a candle or lantern.

"Simply wonderful," she gushed, shaking her head as they left the den. "I am very impressed with your home."

"I wish I hadn't been looking at it for the last thirty years," Dwight quipped. "Other than the years I was gone, of course. None of this is new to me, and I'm afraid much of the beauty has been lost to these eyes. Nothing here is unique to me. I'm only trying to maintain what my father put in place."

Dwight sounded completely genuine and honest to Belinda. Through their tour, he'd relayed anecdotes featuring him as a young man in that great mansion of space, seeing how fast he could run down the long hallway that was split by the huge stairwell going up to the second floor. He'd slid down the banister and gone flying toward the front door many times in his life. Sometimes, he said, he landed on his feet and felt like the most triumphant acrobat in all the world.

Belinda couldn't help laughing when she pictured that.

He'd been a bit quiet in the office, but she didn't ask why. She felt she knew the answer. It probably reminded him of his father. Belinda had no doubt that five years wasn't really enough time for someone not to feel a heavy sorrow at the loss of a loved one, especially a parent or child.

She respected his need for privacy and didn't pry into that subject. It would probably come up at some point because she already planned to tell him she knew about the rumors that had put disgrace upon his name. She didn't know how she was going to work it in that she knew, though. That's why she was waiting. She wouldn't just blurt it out. That would lead to several questions she didn't want to answer quite yet.

"Let's go for a walk in the garden after I show you your room," Dwight suggested in an enthused voice. "You'll love the flowers. You'll notice that we grow them here, and they supply all of our vases with beauty every other day."

"Lovely," Belinda breathed.

She and Dwight went up the stairs side by side. He turned to the right when he got to the top, holding his hand out for her to go in that direction. She did and ascended that flight of stairs to the landing.

He passed her with a simple grin and gestured to the first door on their left. "This is my room. I hope you don't mind, but I'm not going to show you the inside."

Belinda blushed and shook her head with a little smile crossing her lips. "No, that's okay. My room is fine. I'll just imagine what's behind that door." Her blush deepened. Her face was boiling hot. She couldn't believe she'd just said that. Hearing Dwight's soft chuckle when he turned to lead her to her room didn't make it any easier for her to forgive herself for the blunder.

"This is the room. It's next to my room, but it's large on the inside, so you won't feel cramped."

Belinda wasn't sure why he thought she would be cramped. He opened the door and let her go in first.

She was just as impressed with the room she was being given as she was with everything else she'd seen. She turned in another slow circle. "Oh my. This is very nice, Dwight. Thank you. Did you know I was coming? You've chosen my favorite colors in here."

Dwight lifted his eyebrows, his face brightening. "I didn't know you were coming, I promise you. I'm glad you like it."

The room also sported flowers. They were a subtle, soft orange that went well with the yellow, off-white, white, and baby blue spread throughout.

"I can definitely sleep here," she said, nodding with approval.

"Wonderful. Go ahead and leave your bag here. Let's go look around outside. I'm anxious to show you my flower garden."

Belinda followed Dwight out the door, thinking how comfortable she already was with him. She didn't see a criminal when she looked at him. She was determined to clear his name, feeling the same trustworthiness in him that Lionel felt. He would have to be a superior actor for his behavior and actions not to be genuine.

14

———

By the time dinnertime rolled around, Belinda was sure she was safe at the ranch and with Dwight. She found herself missing Lionel and wished he lived in the bunkhouse so she could see him all the time. Dwight had informed her that Lionel was the mayor's son—which she already knew—and that he had been doing free work for Dwight because of some recent trouble they'd been having.

Belinda decided not to bring the subject back up until they were seated at the dinner table, which was actually quite long and had room for ten counting the seats at the ends. Dwight sat at the end, and Belinda took the seat to his right. The cook brought in the trays, and the maid served them both. They were quiet during that time.

When the maid went back to the kitchen, Belinda took a few bites and nodded when he offered to pour her a glass of wine. She waited just a few minutes so they could get settled in before she spoke.

"Earlier, you said that Lionel was helping out around here because of some trouble you've been having. I hope it's not impolite for me to ask you more about that. I know I intruded on your privacy, but I always think it's a good idea to know what kind of situation I'm getting myself into. I need to know all I can about my surroundings, you see."

Dwight nodded energetically, picking up his wine glass and holding it in front of him while he spoke. He took intervals to take a sip from it before continuing.

"I completely understand. That is a good way to think. Very intelligent."

Belinda felt her chest squeeze as it usually did when she was genuinely complimented.

"I find myself in a spot of trouble, yes. There has been some cattle rustling going on at the nearby ranches. Sabotage being committed by people as yet unknown. Some of the people in this county are sure it is my work."

Belinda was a little surprised at how easily he said those words. She noticed he did take a gulp of wine right after saying them.

"I am not responsible for the cattle rustling. Let me make that clear to you right now. If you feel I am that kind of man, I invite you not to stay."

Belinda shook her head. "From what I've seen so far today, I do not believe you would be capable of something like that. You don't seem like a criminal to me. But please, why are they saying you are responsible? Why would anyone think that?"

Dwight was hesitant. He took a deep breath and let it out through his nose, pinching his lips together. He took another big gulp of his wine, and his eyes were out the window when he responded. Belinda could almost see him reliving what happened as he relayed it to her.

"I left home when I was twenty years old. I was gone for five years. My pa became deathly ill after being poisoned by a spider. He never recovered and died six months after he was bitten. During that time, I was on a boat in the middle of the ocean. His letters did not reach me until I returned, which happened to be..." He hesitated and swallowed hard. His eyes dropped to his wine glass and swirled the liquid gently, "it was the day he died. That's when I returned to my home in New York. I saw the letters that had piled up while I was unreachable. I was on the first train back and did not get here until days after he died. I didn't even know he was gone when I got here."

"Oh, my," Belinda murmured gently, her heart going out to the man. "I'm so sorry."

"When I stepped off that train, I was immediately met with glares and anger. People were so upset that I hadn't come home before he died. The rumor started that I was only here to claim my inheritance and that I'd never cared for my father in the first place."

Belinda frowned. She almost asked a question that would have given away her previous knowledge of the situation, but she caught herself and reformed it. "Weren't you... Didn't people know you before you left? If you were twenty, the folks in this county should have already known you were a... What kind of man you really are. You were an adult. You didn't leave when you were a child."

"I reckon in the eyes of some of these folks, I was a child. Or I was not sincere in my concern and love for my father before I left. Some have said that I left because of a rift with my father, and that's why I stayed away. That is patently untrue."

Belinda was surprised to feel a pang of irritation at the county people harassing Dwight. He had a perfectly valid reason for what happened. For someone to think his reason was a lie, they would have already had to bear some animosity toward him.

She listened to his frustration, letting her mind wander on the topic of her plans for discovering the truth behind the matter. He was being framed for the cattle rustling while still experiencing sabotage on his own property.

When she felt he'd ranted himself out, and he stopped to contemplate all he'd said, she took the opportunity to speak.

"And you are experiencing sabotage here?"

Dwight nodded. He stabbed his fork in the slice of turkey on his plate, but instead of picking it up, he stabbed it a few more times. "The only men who would be investigating this believe I'm lying. They think that if I would lie about not being able to come back in time to see my father before his death, I would definitely lie to keep myself out of trouble for cattle rustling. I would lose everything. I will lose everything." His voice shook with emotion.

Belinda couldn't help herself. She reached out to him and rested her hand on his arm. He gave her a grateful look and sighed.

"I'm sorry you have walked into this. I hope it doesn't affect you in any way. I may actually be glad to have you here. I might have to marry you from a jail cell, and you can take everything over. I don't know how long they'll put me in prison if I'm found guilty."

Belinda shook her head. "Don't talk like that. You aren't going to be found guilty. You haven't even been charged yet. There will be people working on your side. Lionel seems influential. Surely he is helping you."

"Lionel is a great help, yes. He's my best friend. He says he has a brilliant mind on the case. I hope the man discovers the truth soon. I don't know how much longer I've got till my freedom is taken away. I don't think cattle rustling is punishable by death, but I feel like there are men in town who would like to see that happen."

"How ghoulish," Belinda grumbled, once again irritated with the sheriff, the inspector, the mayor, and anyone else who thought Dwight was responsible for the criminal actions. "How long has this been going on?"

"About six months."

"How many times has it happened?"

Dwight appeared thoughtful. "I reckon the cattle theft has happened about once, maybe twice a month. Not sure of the numbers. I don't know about sabotage on the other farms, but in the last three months, I can't tell you how many times we've found damaged fences, deep holes dug where they shouldn't be, let out two of the bulls. The list goes on and on." He shook his head, grabbing his napkin and wiping his mouth. He dropped the napkin on his half-empty plate, signifying he was done with his food.

Belinda's first thought was to tell him he should eat more to keep up his strength. She didn't need to have seen Dwight before all this started to know he was looking deflated. Defeated. It wasn't right, in her opinion. She intended to do everything she could to prove Dwight innocent of the charges and to restore his happiness in life.

And although she felt her heart turn toward Dwight, she knew it was only friendship she would feel for him. With Lionel, however, it was a different story.

15

Lionel rode his horse around the pasture one more time just to make sure the fence was complete and intact. If it was busted in the morning, they would know it was done on purpose. The weather was perfect for the season—no expected rain, wind, or other problems that could cause damage to the property.

He turned Champion in the direction of the ranch house with the intention of heading home. What he really wanted to do was see Belinda. He ached to talk to her about what was going on and if she'd made any progress on her end that day. He reimagined her emerging from the woods on her horse, looking so innocent. It always made him smile.

The sky had darkened, and he was using a lantern that he'd affixed to a long pole that was then secured to the horn on his saddle. It stretched out over the top of the horse's head and lit the way. He was beside the chow house and couldn't help looking at the huge residence he was about to pass.

Through a window, he saw a bright lantern burning. It silhouetted a female figure, who appeared to be sitting in the window seat, head down, as if reading a book on her lap.

Lionel's heart jumped with excitement. He turned his horse and headed toward the window, knowing Belinda was in the parlor. He couldn't wait to ask her what she'd discovered.

He rode over to the window and stopped by it, leaning down to slap his reins against the glass. She looked up in surprise. When she saw him, her face lit up. He derived a little pleasure from that look and smiled at her.

She fiddled with the latch on the window and then rolled it open, leaning out into the cool night air.

"Lionel. What are you doing here?"

Lionel raised his eyebrows. "Don't tell me he didn't tell you I do patrols around the property in the evening before I head back to the mansion."

She grinned. "Oh. Well, he said you were helping out. He didn't say how specifically."

"Nice to know you two are talking about me," he quipped. "What's your opinion so far? You didn't end up telling him who you really are, did you?"

Belinda let out a pleasant laugh. "No. But I had a mind to just come out and tell him. I'm afraid he won't be as genuine with me after, though. I want to find out who is doing this to him and who the real cattle rustlers are before I tell him who I am. I worry that he will be angry at the deception."

"It's for a good cause," Lionel reminded her. "He might be angry at first, but he will forgive you."

Belinda grunted in a humorous way that made Lionel chuckle. "Only if we find out who is guilty first. He told me why he didn't come back for his father, by the way. You didn't tell me about that."

Lionel nodded, hoping she wouldn't be angry about his withholding information. "I really felt like that was something he needed to tell you."

"Well, he did. And I don't understand why the men in town don't believe him. It sounds perfectly plausible to me. And the way he speaks of his father and how devastated he was not to get those letters until it was far too late." She shook her head. "I could tell how horrible he felt about it. I would, too.

And to top it all off, he has to live the rest of his life with the knowledge that he didn't get to really say goodbye."

Lionel agreed with her, thinking about how his friend was nearly depleted after five years of trying to be strong. "He's shouldered these burdens and the hatred of others for so long now," he remarked. "I've grown very tired of it."

"I do have a question, though," Belinda said, leaning down so she had her arms crossed on the window sill and her body was leaning halfway out resting on them.

"Please go ahead and ask."

"Why now? Why are they doing this now?"

"That's a really good question." Lionel hadn't even thought about that before. If someone wanted to take revenge on Dwight, wouldn't they have done it the moment he came back? Or started their scheme a short time after he came back to imply he was guilty even more? "I don't know the answer to that. I guess when we find out who is doing it, we'll find out their reasoning."

Belinda moved her lips around, biting them together and licking them as she thought. Her eyes roamed around beyond Dwight. He, however, kept his eyes on her. He wished he could hear her thoughts. He was interested to know how her thought process worked.

"Still... that's one of the things that, if we were able to determine, we'd be able to narrow down the field a lot. It would serve as a motive for the set-up so the sheriff and the rest would have to look away from Dwight instead of at him. We also need to find out who has been given enough time from their employers to be out cattle rustling. This isn't just the job of one man. There are many men involved with one mastermind. Obviously, we're looking for the mastermind, but the underlings will lead us to the real criminal at the top."

Lionel nodded, watching her face as she worked through it. His admiration grew for her every time he had a chance to talk to her.

"I know you'll figure it out," he said encouragingly. "What's your plan from here on out? You obviously think he's innocent. What will you do now?"

"I want to look through Dwight's office. I don't know what I might find there, but I know that's the first place to start looking. I need to see his financial records and any schedule he's kept a record of. If we can determine where he was during certain episodes of sabotage or rustling, that would clear him. But not completely. They think he's behind it. They haven't said he's actually participating. He's the man with the money directing everyone to do the crimes."

"Or so they say."

Belinda's eyes darted up to him like she'd forgotten she was talking to him. It was amusing, and he gave her a playful grin. Her face softened, and she smiled at him.

"How about you come back in the morning and we'll talk? Dwight mentioned at dinner that he has an appointment in town at nine. He said I could do whatever I wanted while he was gone. He certainly is a trusting soul. I could go through here and take everything he has of value."

"That works good for us," Lionel said, "but it's definitely one of the things I've been protecting him from for many years. I've been trying to protect him. He never took a dime from me nor I him. We are like brothers. We care about each other."

Belinda nodded. "I can tell. I'm glad he has you as a friend. I think if he didn't, he would be very alone."

"I agree. He would have tried to find a woman to be on his arm without anyone to warn him and make sure he isn't choosing beauty over brains. That's really never good unless you are wanting to create drama and pain for yourself."

Belinda screwed her face up at him. "And no one wants that." She turned abruptly and looked behind her. "I think I heard him," she said anxiously, spinning back to put her hand on the window handle. She began to turn it, and the window rolled closed. "Tomorrow at nine," she said right before the door closed. He nodded and rode away immediately, catching out of the corner of his eye when Dwight opened the door and spotted her on the window seat.

He would be back at nine the next morning.

16

Belinda had just sat back down and dropped her eyes to the book when Dwight pushed open the door and entered. It was late, and she'd thought he was already asleep. When he saw her, he reacted with such surprise, his entire body jerked. She could see by his half-closed eyes and slightly swollen face that he'd been asleep and had just woken up. He was carrying a cup with steaming liquid in it.

"I—I'm sorry. I forgot you were here." He closed his eyes and covered them with one hand. "I didn't mean... I..."

"It's all right," Belinda said in a forgiving voice. She set her book aside and got up, moving toward him. "I am the one who should be sorry. I've intruded on your privacy. I'm sorry. I'll get to bed. Unless you'd like to talk."

He ran his hand through his hair and shook it. "I don't mind if you stay. It would be nice to have someone to talk to. It's been a long time. Other than Lionel, I've been pretty much alone for the past five years."

"That's a long time to feel alone," Belinda responded sympathetically. She put one hand on his arm and directed him gently to the couch. "I'm here now. I'll listen if you want to talk." Even if she hadn't been there for investigative purposes, Belinda would have offered a listening ear.

When Dwight dropped to the couch, it was as if he weighed a thousand pounds. His shoulders slumped, and his head lowered. He took a sip of what Belinda could tell was hot cocoa. Her taste buds longed for some of the delicious drink, but she wasn't about to ask for a minute to go make a cup. He needed her at that moment.

She ran one hand over his back comfortingly.

"What's on your mind right now?" she asked softly.

He didn't answer right away. Belinda saw his jaw clench. Her heart went out to him.

"My pa," he finally answered, his voice so low she

could barely hear him. She took her hand from his back and clasped them in front of her, looking down so that she would be staring. "I wonder if he understood. If he was angry with me for never writing back. I..." He stopped, his voice breaking. "I hope he went to Heaven and God let him know that I would have come back."

Belinda gave him a soft look and leaned slightly against him to let him know she was there and listening. He pinched the bridge of his nose between his fingers, squeezing his eyes shut. It didn't stop the flow of tears from coming through. He sobbed quietly for a few minutes while Belinda wrapped her arms around his shoulders and held on to him.

"I should never have gone on that trip. Whatever the reason, it wasn't worth the result."

"Why did you go on it? Where was your destination?"

Dwight gulped and hiccupped, getting himself back under control slowly. He pulled in a deep breath. He pressed his hands together and swallowed. "I went on a mission trip to South Africa."

Belinda pulled back from him a little, tilting her head to the side. "A mission trip? Are you a preacher of some kind?"

"No," he said, shaking his head. "It was to bring

food and supplies to several villages where people were starving. Children. Women with child. The older folks. I thought I was doing the right thing."

Belinda felt a surge of admiration mixed with compassion flood her body. "You did do the right thing. You must have told your father you were going. Surely you told him."

Dwight said nothing, but he confirmed her suspicion by nodding his head.

She gripped him hard and spoke with passion, "Then he knew you might be unreachable. He must have spoken to people before he passed, friends, his doctor. Someone has to know what mood he was in and what he was thinking. Have you asked?"

Dwight shook his head. "The only people who would tell me wouldn't talk to me."

"But surely he must have told them."

Dwight moved his head and gave her a sad look. "If he did, they aren't acknowledging it. I told them when I got back the reason for my delay, and they didn't accept that reason."

"Why would he have kept it to himself?" Belinda asked softly.

Dwight returned his eyes to his clasped hands. "I don't know."

"Do you really think he would have? He wouldn't

have wanted everyone to reject you or think badly of you. He would have told them."

Belinda couldn't believe that so many of Dwight and his father's friends chose to believe the worst possible thing about Dwight. He seemed like such a quiet, sweet man. How could they watch him grow up and think such a horrible thing about him?

"I would have thought so," he said softly, "but even if he did, they aren't accepting either his or my explanation. And there's nothing I can do to change their minds. I could save a bunch of children from a burning building, and they would say I did it to get attention."

Belinda shook her head, frowning, feeling frustration for him. "I just don't understand that. It doesn't make sense to me. You told your father where you were going. It was nothing but a coincidence that he was bitten by that spider while you were on a boat sailing to Africa. I am sure your father loved you. I can tell by how much you loved him that he must have been very good to you. He wouldn't have been if he didn't love you as much as he did."

Dwight was silent, his eyes down. He splayed his fingers, pressing his fingertips together. He was breathing more normally, and his face was returning to its normal color. He glanced at her, tears still in his ears. "He did love me a lot. He was a wonderful father. I'm the man I am today because of him."

"And a fine gentleman you turned out to be," Belinda replied encouragingly. "Don't you ever doubt that your father loved you. You know better than that. He's up there in Heaven shaking his head at you for thinking otherwise." She gave him a warm smile.

He chuckled under his breath, smiling back at her. When he turned his head back to look at the floor once more, Belinda tilted her head toward his, resting her cheek on his shoulder. He responded by leaning his head against hers.

Belinda closed her eyes. She hoped she had helped him feel better.

He patted her hand on his arm before reaching toward his hot cocoa. He grasped the side and then let go, saying, "Cold. I think I'll just head back to bed. Thanks for listening to me, Belinda. You really helped. I appreciate it."

"Anytime, Dwight," she whispered, lifting her head to look at him. "I'm heading to bed myself. Everything will be better in the morning. You wait and see."

Dwight didn't look at her when he said, "With

you here, I think things will be better for a long time." He glanced at her. "As long as you want to stay, though. Don't ever think I'm forcing you. I don't want you to feel controlled. I'm not that kind of man and wouldn't be that kind of husband."

"I'm sure you wouldn't, Dwight," Belinda replied, squeezing his muscular arm. "And I'm not at all worried about it."

He stood up, and she took his hand when he offered it. She used it to pull herself to her feet.

"Good night," he said, leaning forward, taking both her hands in his.

She squeezed his hands when he did the same.

"Good night, Dwight. Sweet dreams."

17

Lionel showed up at nine on the dot.

When Belinda opened the door, she surprised him by sticking her head out and looking in the direction of the bunkhouse. She reached out and pulled him in by his sleeve.

"Get in here," she said anxiously. When he was inside, she closed the door and put her back against it, laying her hands flat against the wood behind her, looking up at him. He was amused and lifted one side of his lips in a half-grin.

"What are you doing?" he asked curiously.

"I'm quite sure the men know that Dwight isn't here this morning. After breakfast, he went out to work on the barn until eight. His appointment is at nine. He cleaned up and left at eight-thirty. If they see you come in here when I'm alone, they might get ideas. I don't want that to happen." She looked around, her eyes dodging from one side to the other. "It's bad enough we have to avoid the servants."

Lionel was highly amused by her concern. "Oh, I thought I told you," he said. "I'm a local hero. No one thinks anything bad of me."

Belinda gave him a look. "Oh, we are confident, aren't we?"

He shrugged, squeezing the rim of his hand in his hand. He felt a pang of regret, hoping she didn't think he was boastful. He got the impression she didn't when she grabbed his arm and darted down the hallway toward Dwight's study.

"Let's get in his study as quick as we can. I don't want anyone seeing us. I have to worry about what they will think of me. They might not think bad of you, but no one in Josephson County knows me at all."

"If I'm with you, there's no threat to your reputation unless I was to go around telling everyone you were flirting with me when Dwight isn't around. And there's no chance I would do anything like that. No chance at all."

Belinda opened the door to Dwight's study, and the two of them slipped through, closing the door quietly behind them. Belinda locked it while Dwight looked on, entertained by her stealthy movements.

Once the door was locked, though, she seemed to relax. She turned in a slow circle.

Lionel had been in his friend's office the day before. He was regularly there and knew what was around him. He'd never gone through his friend's things, though, and told himself he was doing it for Dwight's good and not for any other reason.

"I guess I'll start with the desk. You check the cabinet with the files." Belinda went around and sat in Dwight's chair.

Lionel wondered if she was as nervous about what they were doing as he was.

"You know," he said, pulling the top drawer of the cabinet open and fingering through the folders sitting upright inside, "I've asked him so many questions about this sabotage business, I just don't know what we could possibly find in here. He isn't involved. I would know. I spend most of my free time with him. I can't imagine him making sure he has time to run off when I'm not around so he can steal cattle and sabotage other ranches."

"Well, you aren't here at night when the crimes are actually being committed," Belinda pointed out. She looked up at him while shuffling through the drawer to her immediate left, which she'd pulled open first. "I'm not saying he's involved. I'm just saying you aren't with him all night long. Those who think he is involved will bring that up and say you don't know."

"Frustrating, to say the least." Lionel closed the drawer and pulled open the one underneath it. It was filled with ledgers laid flat. He saw the year at the date embedded in gold numbers. He didn't see the year 1850 and assumed it must be in the desk currently being used. He closed the drawer, as nothing in those ledgers would have anything to do with the last six months.

"Lionel, come look at this," Belinda said, her voice alarmed. His eyes darted to her. She had the bottom drawer open and looked up at him with worry on her face.

That expression sent concern burning through Lionel's chest. He hurried over and leaned to see what was in the drawer. It looked like balled-up papers. Belinda had pulled one out and flattened it so she could see what it said.

Chills ran over his skin. He held out his hand, and she gave it to him. He stared at the words on the paper.

"Your time is coming," he read. The four words

reinvigorated the chill he'd felt a few seconds before. He moved his eyes to the rest of the balled-up papers. "Do they all say this?"

Belinda began to pull them out, flattening them on the desk. Each one was threatening, but they did not all say the same thing. He counted the last one at eight when she pressed it flat.

"I don't believe this," Lionel said in a low voice, shaking his head. "He told me he didn't know who was doing this. He said no one was threatening him."

Belinda raised her eyebrows, turning her head to look up at him. "He told you no one was threatening him? Or that he didn't know who it was? Because it seems to me he knows he's being threatened. With the sabotage and these threats, we all know someone is out to get him. But none of these are signed, and he obviously doesn't know where they came from."

Lionel's heart thumped hard in his chest. "I told him to tell me. I asked him over and over. He never told me about these."

"Maybe he's ashamed."

Belinda surprised him once again by snatching the paper in his hands and balling it up. She dropped it down in the deep drawer and picked the rest up, one by one, balling them up and dropping them back down.

"That was him that came in the parlor last night after you left. He was in quite a state. I held on to him, hugged him, comforted him. Not being able to say goodbye to his father really bothers him so very much. I don't believe for a minute that he is involved in these thefts or the sabotage."

"I don't either," Lionel said, giving her a close look. "I reckon you don't want us to confront him with these threatening notes, huh?"

Belinda shook her head. "No. He was so broken-hearted last night. I really think he is ashamed and overwhelmed. I almost wish I had been writing to him and had fallen in love with him. He needs someone. He needs a woman who loves him to help ease his pain."

"Do you think that might be you?" Lionel asked. For some reason, in the back of his mind, he was hoping she would say no.

She shook her head, and he was relieved.

"No. He's... a good man—a gentleman. But I didn't feel a pull to him. No spark between us, I think. He's a bit docile, and I'm looking for energy and vibrance." She gave him a friendly grin. "I know he's a nice fellow, but I doubt he was ever really full of vim and vigor. He said that he went on a missionary trip to Africa, and that sounded like exactly the kind of thing I would expect from him, even after only knowing him for a day."

Lionel nodded. "He cares more about other people than he does himself. I know this is a huge burden on him. He never got to grieve his father. He felt so guilty for so long."

"What's this?" Belinda had closed the drawer with the balled-up letters and pulled the middle drawer toward her chest. There was a letter there, face up.

"That's a letter from his lawyer," Lionel replied, spotting the return address. "I don't think we need to be reading that. That seems like a bit much, don't you think?"

He was glad when Belinda nodded, pushing the drawer closed.

"Yes. I agree. His business. It would be wrong."

"I feel bad enough about what we've done, but I wish he had told me about the letters."

"What do you think we should do now?" Belinda asked, standing up. "I think we've done enough in here, don't you?"

"Yes. I think we should pay a visit to his lawyer, Mr. Clingenpeel. He was a friend of Tom's, too, but he was fully aware of Dwight's reason for being so delayed, and he never held it against him."

"Good. But will he talk to us?"

Lionel nodded, feeling confident he was right. "He's a friend of mine, too, and he likes Dwight. He'll talk to us."

18

They were in the foyer when they heard the sound of a horse approaching outside. Belinda gave Lionel a wary look, which he returned. She hurried to the door and went through to see Dwight approaching. He looked depressed. Her heart went out to him, and she quickly moved to the steps to go down to him.

Belinda would never know what she stepped on that made her lose her balance. Maybe her ankle just rolled. Maybe the hem of her skirt got caught under her foot. Whatever it was, she found herself tipping forward, nothing to grab onto and the hard steps coming straight for her face.

Before she could fall far, though, two hands wrapped around her waist and yanked her back. She was promptly set back on her feet but then tipped backward, falling into Lionel's arms.

Fear had filled her mind, and she looked up at Lionel with eyes as wide as saucers.

"I'm so... so sorry," she exclaimed, pushing at his hands and trying desperately to stand back up on her own. "I..."

"Hush," Lionel said in a voice so low and smooth, Belinda promptly forgot that she had just been about to smash her face on the steps. She stared at him. Her body felt suddenly hot, and she relaxed against him. He gently placed her on her feet. He didn't take his eyes from hers.

Something changed at that moment. The feelings that had been lying underneath the surface decided to make an appearance. She'd thought he was a handsome man from the start. At that moment, it was like she saw past the surface to what was hidden deep underneath. She could see it in his eyes. Her heart jumped into overdrive.

Belinda had to force herself to get her emotions under control. This was not the time to be falling in love. Maybe when all of this was over, she could venture into that realm. But she had to concentrate on important things right now. A distraction was not wanted.

Unfortunately, there was nothing she could do about it. She was done for.

She brushed her hands over her dress and cleared her throat.

"Thank you," she said, finally tearing her eyes away from him. He was still looking at her, though.

Dwight had left his horse at the stable and was heading toward them, his head down, his shoulders slumped.

"Oh dear," she murmured, seeing his state. "He's unwell. We need to get him inside."

"This whole thing is weighing heavily on him," Lionel remarked, agreeing with her. "It hurts me to see him being destroyed. Five years this has been going on. Now it's coming to a head."

"I'm glad you've been here for him," Belinda said over her shoulder as she went down the steps.

A few minutes later, she was next to Dwight, one arm around his waist, her eyes up and scanning his face. "What's happened, Dwight? Are you all right?"

"I don't want to talk about it," Dwight replied in a dark voice. "I just want to go inside."

"I'll make you something to eat and fix you a drink."

"Thank you, Belinda. I appreciate your help." He

looked up. "Lionel," he greeted his friend, holding out his hand.

"You're lookin' pretty rough, buddy. You gonna be all right?"

"That remains to be seen," Dwight replied. "You want a drink?"

Lionel nodded. "Yeah, I'm okay with that. I don't have much of anything to do today."

"You come to make sure everything was safe and secure with the ranch while I was gone?"

The three walked in the house together, Belinda going in first and heading to the kitchen to make the man something to eat.

Betty, the cook, was standing at the oven, using a large mitt to pull a tray of cookies from the heat. She turned and saw Belinda.

"Good afternoon, Miss," she said pleasantly.

"Is it afternoon already?"

"Just after twelve, yes, Miss," Betty responded.

"Well, good afternoon then. I need to have a quick lunch made for Dwight. He had just returned and is looking a little worse for wear."

"Oh, dear." Betty hurried to the counter near the icebox. She made ham and cheese sandwiches, placed several pickles on a plate, and put together another with apple, orange, and banana slices alongside a bunch of grapes. Belinda watched her, talking while she worked.

"Do you like working for Dwight?"

"I do," Betty replied with a nod. "He is a kind man."

"Did you work for his father, too?"

"I did, yes. He was also a kind man. I've been here for nearly ten years now. I remember when Dwight left. Tom missed him so very much. But they did correspond. They wrote on a regular basis. I know because I posted the letters for Tom."

Belinda nodded, tilting her head to the side. "Do you think Tom was upset that Dwight didn't come back while he was ill?"

Without missing a beat, Betty snorted and shook her head. "How could he not be upset that he couldn't be with his son during such a horrible time? Did he hold it against Dwight? No. He knew his son was living his life and knew Dwight was unreachable for that entire six months he was on the trip to Africa. He loved his son. I know Dwight feels guilty, but I think that's mostly because of the men in town who are so unreasonable. It makes me very angry."

Belinda was impressed with the woman. Betty looked like she was around the age of her parents. She was plump and curvy but tall enough not to look round and fat. She pulled a large tray from a cabinet and set the food on it before handing the entire thing to Belinda.

"You tell him he is loved. That's all he needs to know. I wish I could tell him, but I work for him, and I'm afraid he will take it the wrong way. He is like a son to me."

"I understand." Belinda took the tray, smiling at the woman. "I'll tell him he's loved. I have no problem doing that."

"Thank you, Miss. I'm glad you're here. He needs a new friend."

When she left the kitchen, Belinda contemplated with the cook had said. Dwight just needed to be loved. He was lonely. She completely understood his need to reach out through the ads, get away from the stigma of what had happened and the sneering looks of some of the men in town. She imagined he had encountered one of those men. That was probably what had caused this new bout of depression.

She entered the parlor and saw that Lionel had made them both a couple of stiff drinks. They were sitting in two chairs that were angled toward each other. Lionel was leaning on the armrest closer to his friend, his eyes on Dwight, listening intently to what his friend was saying.

Both men stood up when she entered, and Dwight's words abruptly stopped.

Belinda set the tray down on the coffee table near them, picked up the plate of sandwiches, and offered it to one and then the other. Both took two sandwiches each.

"Thank you for this, Belinda." Dwight gave her a shaky smile.

She smiled back warmly, saying, "I didn't make any of this. It was your nice cook, Betty, who did it. I am merely the messenger."

"And for that, I am grateful," Dwight responded.

"You're welcome, Dwight. I want you to feel better."

19

Lionel and Belinda took their own horses to town. Along the way, Lionel found himself struggling to keep his mind on the task at hand.

When he'd caught Belinda and kept her from falling down the steps, it was like he'd been struck by Cupid's arrow. He looked into her eyes, and it seemed she reached into his chest and pulled his heart out. Suddenly, she was the most beautiful woman he'd ever seen. Not that he'd thought she was ugly before that moment. He'd always thought she was pretty. He knew he'd been admiring her from the beginning.

But now—it was overwhelming. He'd felt this

way only once before, with a girl he'd gone to the schoolhouse with. She was similar in looks and personality to Belinda. But that young lady had contracted influenza and passed at the age of eighteen before Lionel could ever tell her how he felt about her. She'd spent the last two years of her life fighting illness after illness until she was gone.

His feelings for Belinda were very much the same as that first love he'd had.

He glanced at her. She was riding along, not looking at him. He wished they had taken the buggy. He wanted to be seated next to her, to feel her arm brush against his, to hear her breathing or talking to him.

Lionel chided himself for his thoughts. There were many more important things to be done at that moment. He couldn't afford to be distracted. His best friend was about to be charged with a crime he wasn't involved in. He had important tasks to be focused on.

But even as those thoughts ran through his mind, Lionel knew he was already gone. She had taken his heart. There was nothing he could do about it now. He would have to proceed with caution so that he didn't scare her away with the intensity of his feelings. In his heart and mind, he vowed to take it as easy and slowly as he could.

"So you are sure that Mr. Clingenpeel will help us?"

"I reckon that's gonna depend on what he can answer and what he can't. Some things are private, I'm sure. Confidential."

"Yes, I'm sure," Belinda replied, nodding. "I just worry that he will tell Dwight we are asking questions about this."

Lionel thought about that for a moment. He came to the conclusion that his friend was not going to care at this point. He pictured Dwight's down and out face when he'd returned from town. He sighed.

"It feels like Dwight is just existing right now," he said sorrowfully. "I don't think he'd even care if he knew we were asking questions. He would assume we were trying to help. That's the way he is. He's not going to expect malice until it's right in his face."

Belinda grunted. "The kind of man who tried to pet a snake as a boy."

Lionel turned his head and gazed at her. "Exactly," he responded. He had physically stopped his friend from picking up a snake to pet when they were around nine years old. He still remembered it.

The snake had bitten him instead when he slapped it out of his friend's hand.

"No good deed goes unpunished," his father had told him.

Lionel tried not to have such a negative outlook on things.

They got to the lawyer's office ten minutes later and left their horses along the side of the building where there were water troughs with clear water in them.

Lionel could tell Belinda was a bit nervous as they walked around to the front of the building. He didn't knock but just opened the door and held it for Belinda , allowing her to pass in front of him and go in first.

The inside was bright, the walls white and everything around her was gold-plated. She had to assume it was that way because if he was showcasing lamps and doorknobs made of gold, it was an unreasonable excess in Belinda's opinion. The interior smelled heavily of roses, most likely due to the fact that every single vase she saw had at least a dozen roses in it. She thought it was likely there were several rose bushes growing on someone's property that allowed them to bring in fresh ones on a regular basis.

"Through here," Lionel said, waving one hand at her. She followed him to the door that said "Clingenpeel" on the front and entered when he turned the knob and pushed the door open.

The man behind the huge thick wood desk looked up when they came in. Thick, black-rimmed eyeglasses fronted his eyes, and a heavy black mustache topped his upper lip.

He stood up, his eyes sliding from one of them to the other.

"Lionel Calverson. How are you, son? Come on in. And who is this lovely lady?"

Belinda spoke up before Lionel could say anything, and her words came as a surprise to him. Still, he was as impressed as ever with her when she was finished.

"I think you might have known my uncle," she said quickly, glancing at Lionel with an apologetic look. "Gabriel Salinger? I'm Belinda , his niece. We took over the Wagon Wheel Justice Agency a few years ago. Well, almost. I think I remember seeing your name in his files."

"Why yes, I do remember Mr. Salinger. I only worked with him on, I believe, one or two cases. No more than three."

Belinda smiled and shook her head. "I wouldn't

know how many. I just remember seeing your last name on some documents, and I was wondering if it was you or not."

"Yes, that would be me."

Mr. Clingenpeel came around his desk, holding out his hand. He was dressed immaculately and had on a gold necklace, bracelet, and flashy cuff links.

Lionel shook his hand after Belinda , and the two of them sat down.

"I'm relieved that you knew her uncle," Lionel said. "We've been doing some of our own investigating on this case of cattle rustling and sabotage. Dwight has spoken to you about it, hasn't he?"

"Actually," Mr. Clingenpeel replied, rounding his desk again so he could sit in his chair again, "I'm glad you've come by, Lionel. I know you are very close to him."

Lionel nodded, feeling a pinch of sentiment in his chest. "He's my best friend," he said plainly.

Mr. Clingenpeel nodded. "Yes, I know. And I've wanted to express my concern over his apparent depressed state." He hesitated and rested his eyes directly on Lionel. "I fear for his safety, Lionel."

Chills erupted all over Lionel's body. He swallowed and fought the emotions that welled up in his chest. "My friend is not the type to take his own life," he said.

"And I believe that," the lawyer stated, his voice gentle and concerned, "that does not stop me from believing that the Devil can creep in when a man is most vulnerable."

"That's not going to happen," Lionel announced in a loud voice. "Belinda is here to help him. He will see that there is plenty of life to be had." He suddenly had the urge to go back to Big T Ranch, grab his friend, and lock him in a secure room—a comfortable one—to keep him from hurting himself. The thought had not crossed his mind until the lawyer brought it up.

"I simply wanted to express my fear to you," Mr. Clingenpeel replied. "And now that you are aware of it, you will feel tasked to keep a closer eye on him, even closer than you've already been. And I'm sure that's very close."

Lionel had noticed Dwight's depressed behavior. At first, he'd thought it was because of his father and that situation. Then it was the cattle rustling and the sabotage. And now Belinda had appeared, and she was deceiving him about who she really was.

Lionel flushed, feeling responsible for adding to

Dwight's humiliation and pain. It was too late to call it off, though, and he was determined to see it through. He just had to pray that things would work out the right way.

20

"We're here to ask if there's anything you can tell us to help us figure out what's going on," Belinda said, unaware that Lionel was going through great inner turmoil at that moment. "You do know what's going on, don't you? He's come and talked to you about it?"

"I have spoken to him, yes." The lawyer got up and crossed to a file cabinet. He pulled open the top drawer and pulled out a folder without really having to look for it. He returned to his desk and unfolded the top to reveal the first document inside. "He was in here two days ago, talking to me about this." He looked up at Belinda. "I was aware of the mail order bride plan he was using to find someone. I encouraged that. I think he is very lonely and needs a companion. Even while he was traveling, he still had a companion."

"I didn't know that," Lionel said, sounding surprised.

Mr. Clingenpeel nodded. "Yes, Moku was a young native boy who ran errands for Dwight and kept him company."

Belinda shared a glance with Lionel. "This is news to me," Lionel said, shaking his head. "Where is this boy now?"

The lawyer's eyebrows shot up. "I assume he went home to his family. He was paid handsomely, enough to set his family up for many years to come. Especially in their native country."

"That's good to know," Lionel remarked. "So, what have you got there?"

"This is a folder I've been making of my own thoughts and discoveries in regards to Dwight's situation." He picked up the top paper and turned it so the two of them could see it. It was a list of dates and times with names in the first column. The lawyer pointed at it, running his finger down the list.

"These are the dates when sabotage occurred around Josephson County. If you look at the pattern here..." He turned his eyes to Belinda. "You have to know the area really well to see the pattern. If I get a map and... hold on."

He got up again and went to a nearby desk. After shuffling through the papers there, he pulled out a map.

Returning to the desk, he pulled open the middle drawer and pulled out a small box of drawing pins. He spread the map out on the desk, placing an object at each corner to keep it flat. Lionel and Belinda stood up to look down at the map.

Belinda could see it covered all of Josephson County. Mr. Clingenpeel took several pins from the box and began to place them around the map, his eyes darting to the page, which he'd set next to the map.

"Here is Big T Ranch." He placed a pin in the area of the map that was Big T property. He used a pen to mark it by writing BT on the map next to the pin. He continued to place the pins, writing initials next to each one of them. He did it in order of the dates when the events had occurred, mumbling what happened when he pushed in the pin. "Sabotage," he mumbled. "Sabotage, cattle theft, sabotage, sabotage, cattle theft."

He looked up at them when the map was well coated with pins.

"Do you see the pattern?" he asked.

Belinda stared at what he'd done. It was just as the inspector had said. The events were happening in a jagged circular pattern around Big T.

"There are two cases of sabotage before a theft and then two more sabotage cases and then a theft," Lionel observed, his voice astonished. "I don't think even the inspector saw that, Bob. Good catch."

"Thank you. I didn't show this to Dwight. I'm not sure he is in the mental state to be dealing with this right now. I'm glad you stopped by. You are the one I wanted to show this to. I would have come to the mayor's mansion, but he is unhappy with me for representing Dwight after Tom." Mr. Clingenpeel looked at Belinda. "I know Dwight was unable to come home. He is a good boy. He was a good boy. Now he is a good man."

Belinda gave the lawyer a warm smile. "I believe you are right."

"There's something else I think you should know, Lionel," the man said, pulling the folder from underneath the map and setting it on top. He shifted through the pages until he found the one he wanted and set it on top of the others.

It was actually a page from the last will and testament of Tom Barnes, which he told Lionel and

Belinda. "In this will, it states that everything goes to Dwight. But there was a stipulation. Tom knew that Dwight would be in Africa. He is aware of the dangers of traveling long distances that way, as well as the general dangers Africa itself poses with neither the natives nor the animals wanting us there except in certain villages that are friendly with America. Like the one he was going to."

The man sat down in the chair again, turning to the side and holding the paper up in the air so they could all see it. The writing was too small for Belinda to see from where she was, but she trusted the lawyer was telling the truth when he spoke.

"Tom and I had many long discussions about what to do if something happened to Dwight on that trip. We discussed this before he was bitten by the spider, before things went downhill for him. He wanted to find someone who would continue the ranch as successful as it is. It was decided, after much discussion, that Mick Lawdry, the foreman, would be given the ranch."

Belinda was stunned. She turned her eyes to Lionel. "You didn't know this before? Dwight didn't tell you?"

"Dwight didn't know," the lawyer answered for Lionel. "It was only to happen if Dwight didn't return for thirty days after the date of his father's death. He returned a few days after Tom died, so there was no need to even bring up the clause. I regret it now. I think Mick might be responsible, at least in part, for what's going on. He may be under the mistaken impression that he will get it if something happens to Dwight. That is incorrect."

"What would happen to the ranch if Dwight was convicted and sent to prison?" Belinda asked.

"It will go to the state, and the mayor will be in control of what happens to it."

Belinda turned her head when Lionel sunk down in his seat, one hand over his face, his eyes closed. She wondered why he had that reaction, though she knew he and his father weren't getting along. Lionel's response still seemed a bit extreme.

"I understand your devastation, Lionel," Mr. Clingenpeel said, apparently understanding better than Belinda did. "Your father has been wanting that land for a while now, hasn't he?"

Lionel nodded without answering or opening his eyes. "I don't want to think Pa could be involved in this," he said, "but I think I might have to consider it."

"I think you should concentrate your efforts on Mick," the lawyer suggested. "The mayor is unaware that the land would be his to control if Dwight goes to prison. As far as I know."

"I agree about Mick," Belinda said, nodding. She looked at Lionel. "We've got a lot to plan out and think about. Let's go get something to eat. We can't think straight on an empty stomach."

Lionel nodded. "Sounds like a good idea."

21

That evening, in his suite in the mayor's mansion, Lionel was surprised by a visit by his father. He was relaxing on the sofa with his feet up, a glass of wine in his hand, and a book in his lap that he wasn't really reading. His mind was filled with thoughts of Dwight and Mick but mostly Belinda. He knew he wouldn't be able to concentrate on the book, but it was a nice cover for what was really on his mind.

The knock on the door prompted him to look up and say, "Come in." He assumed it was his father. No one else ever came to his suite. He always went out, and he wasn't a party-throwing kind of man.

It was his father who walked in.

Jack stopped in the doorway and stared at his

son for a moment before proceeding into the room. He often did that, making Lionel think he thought he looked intimidating. To others, he might have. But Lionel knew his father through and through. He was not a man to be admired or emulated. Lionel went as far away from that attitude and behavior as he could.

Jack came over to a chair near Lionel and dropped down in it. The moment he sat, however, he popped back up and was headed to the bar.

"Make me a strong drink, Pa," he said. "I'm probably going to need it."

"You might."

He returned to the chair a few minutes later, handing a glass of bourbon to his son. Lionel took a sip immediately, wanting to have the relief of a foggy mind while his father complained and demanded.

"What can I do for you, Pa?" he asked, concentrating on the heat of the liquor as it went down his throat and filled his stomach.

"I saw you coming out of Clingenpeel's office earlier today with that woman," his father stated plainly. "Who is she? Why were you in that office?"

Lionel chuckled. "Coming straight to the point. One of the things I like about you, Pa." He hesitated, unsure of how much he wanted to reveal to his father. Thinking his father was involved in the criminal activities going on was almost as disheartening as the accusations against Dwight. Except they were more believable, which made it even harder for Lionel.

"Well, who is she?"

"You're the mayor. Why are you asking me? Shouldn't you know everyone who moves into Josephson County?"

His father narrowed his eyes and gave Lionel a disgruntled look. "Answer my question, please."

Lionel pursed his lips. "Her name is Marie Wright. She's a friend of Dwight's who has come to stay for a while. They might marry."

"Is that so? Is this woman someone he found while traveling?"

"I reckon. He didn't tell me." That was the truth. Dwight didn't know anything about it. Lionel had to look away and lift his glass to his mouth to hide his grin.

"You look very pleased with yourself. I suspect this is a woman you found for him, isn't it?"

"Pa, Dwight's personal life is none of your business. He's my best friend. Not yours. Why do you want to know this?"

Jack grunted. "I like to know all my constituents," he replied.

Lionel snorted. "If that's what you want to claim."

"You are disrespectful." Jack stared at Lionel, his jaw clenched.

Lionel felt a stab of regret. His father had given him everything he had in this life. Unfortunately, that generosity came at a cost. It wasn't heartfelt, genuine giving. It was ensuring that Lionel would owe him when he was older. Jack had taken away Christmas gifts he'd given Lionel when he was a child simply because he made a mistake.

Lots of seven-year-olds make mistakes.

Lionel would never forgive his father for that incident. It still stuck under his skin, irritating him every now and then and fueling his resentment for his father, which was sparked that day.

"I apologize for my rude mouth, Father," Lionel replied. "I'm having trouble understanding why you would show any interest in Dwight or the woman he has with him right now."

"You are looking into the crimes going on, aren't you? You're trying to clear Dwight's name."

Lionel narrowed his eyes at her. "I've been Dwight's best friend since we were small children.

What makes you think I'm not going to try to clear his name? And why shouldn't I?"

"You're going to make things worse for him. You need to leave it to the experts. You shouldn't be bothering anyone with your meddling."

"I'm not meddling. If I were, Clingenpeel would have kicked me out of the office right away. He didn't. He was willing to discuss things with me and, uh, Marie."

He knew his father would catch his hesitation. The man's reaction proved Lionel correct. He sat forward, his eyes focused on his son's face. "Are you telling me the truth, young man?"

Lionel glared at his father. He was not intimidated or afraid. There was nothing the old man could do to him.

"I am telling you what you need to know, Father. I don't have to do what you tell me to do. I haven't needed to for a decade now. I wonder how it would look if you went ahead with your plan and kicked me out? I wonder what your constituents would think of their beloved mayor kicking out the hero who saved all those lives years ago? I wonder what the people whose lives I saved would say if they knew what you really think of me?"

Jack pulled in air through his nose, filling his

chest. "I don't think you know what I think of you," Jack said. "You are my son. I love you."

"You have a very funny way of showing it, Father."

"That's a nice response when you are told you are loved."

Lionel shook his head. "You want me to feel guilty. You don't take your own responsibility for what you do and how you treat others. You aren't as powerful as you think you are, Father. You are just a man. Just like the rest of us."

"I am the mayor," Jack retorted, "and I am your father. The Bible says to honor your father and mother. Do you want to go against what is stated plainly in the Bible?"

Lionel clenched his jaw and closed his eyes for a moment. Was it possible to kick a father from a certain area in his mansion? He desperately wanted to do it right at that moment—physically if he had to.

"Yes, and the Apostle Paul said not to irritate your children."

"He did not say that," Jack snapped.

Lionel's eyebrows shot up. He gave his father an incredulous look. "I beg your pardon. It's in Ephesians. Look it up."

He stood up and walked to the door his father had come through.

"In fact, why don't you go ahead and look that up right now? I have a lot of work to finish and don't have time for meaningless conversations. I'm going to do whatever I can to clear Dwight of these charges that are looming against him. Tom wouldn't have held anything against him. I don't think you have a right to. Please, father. If you wouldn't mind. I am a little busy."

Jack stood up, glaring at Lionel. It was obvious his son wasn't busy with anything, but Lionel didn't care. He didn't want to hear anything more from his father.

After his meeting with the lawyer and hearing that the land would go to the state and its fate controlled by the mayor, he couldn't stop the suspicion from growing in his mind. He didn't know if he would be brave enough to ever snoop in his father's office to search for clues.

Probably not.

Jack stomped to the door and passed by him without another word. He didn't hesitate to close the door once the man was through. He reached down and locked it. He didn't want any interruptions for the rest of the night. It was time to get some rest.

Tomorrow he would discuss their next move with Belinda. They hadn't made any plans to get together, but he would go there in the morning and do another patrol, hopefully seeing Dwight before Belinda.

With a heavy sigh, Lionel retired to his room, praying for solid sleep and a refreshed awakening.

22

Belinda cut the egg white from the yolk with the side of her fork. Dwight was looking a little better this morning. She'd stayed up an extra hour to talk to him and make sure he was comfortable before going to bed herself. She'd woken up refreshed and ready to start the next day.

He was sitting to her left at the head of the table, a newspaper open in front of him. He was eating with a contented look on his face. Belinda felt a measure of gratitude that he appeared to be feeling better.

A knock on the dining room door was followed by Henry coming in. He stood in the doorway, his eyes on Belinda for a moment. Belinda suddenly felt cold from her head to her toes. The older man's eyes slid to Dwight, and he said, "You have a visitor, sir."

He stepped to the side and held out his hand.

A woman came in, walking elegantly past him. She was dressed to the nines, wearing a gorgeous gown, a hat with feathers in it, jewelry around her neck and wrist, and fancy lace-up boots that came up high on her leg, making up for the fairly short length of the dress. Belinda hadn't seen a dress that short since she was on the east coast.

Dwight stood up.

"Howdy," he said, moving from the table and going to the woman with his hand out. She was looking up at him with a confused look on her face. "Dwight Barnes. How may I help you?"

"I'm Fran Lovern," the woman replied in a smooth voice.

Belinda didn't expect the reaction that came next. She had already guessed what was happening and felt for a moment like crawling under the table.

"Fran... Lovern?" Dwight repeated her name slowly. "From the..."

She nodded. "The letters we've been exchanging? You asked me to come."

Dwight pulled in a deep breath and turned to Belinda. "This is Marie Wright. She asks to call her Belinda. Please, won't you join us for breakfast?"

"I don't know if I should."

During this entire exchange, Belinda's face became redder and redder. Her brain was screaming at her to come clean. It was time. She should have already. She trusted Dwight wasn't involved in the crimes. But he had been so emotionally distraught, it had never been a good time to tell him.

She stood up, placing both hands on the surface of the table.

"I have something to confess," she said bluntly.

Dwight and Fran stared at her, both taken aback by her abrupt words. Dwight looked concerned. Belinda herself was concerned. She didn't want to cause Dwight any pain.

"I am not Marie Wright," Belinda blurted out. "My name is Belinda Salinger. My sisters and I run the Wagon Wheel Justice Agency in Sacramento. Lionel approached me last week and asked me to come and investigate the crimes going on here. I assume you sent the letter asking Fran to come before I got here."

She swallowed, turning her eyes away from the

shocked look on Dwight's face and the blank look on Fran's.

"The reason I came undercover was that I wasn't sure you would be open with me, Dwight, and I wanted to know who you really are. I had only ever read about you in the articles Lionel showed to me. I didn't know you. You didn't know me. I wanted to know if you were trustworthy or not."

Dwight's face took on a serious look. Belinda couldn't tell whether he was angry or not.

"And what did you decide?"

Belinda felt like crying. The times she'd comforted Dwight over the past few days ran through her mind. Her concern for him was genuine. It was still genuine.

"You are a good man. You aren't responsible for the crimes. You aren't responsible for the judgment of others, and you would have been here for your father if you could have been. I know that you must be very angry with me right now." She chuckled without humor, shaking her head. "Believe me, Dwight, it was a struggle to reconcile with myself that undercover isn't the highest form of deception. I didn't want to fool you. I had to find out for myself what kind of man you are. Now..." She pulled in a deep breath and gave him a pleading look. "All I want to do is clear your name."

"If you have found love with this woman, I will go back home," Fran said, her voice slightly resentful.

Belinda threw her arms out in front of her, waving her hands back and forth. "No, no," she exclaimed. "No, you must stay. You must. I formed no bond other than friendship with Dwight." She blinked at the man. "Wouldn't you say that we have become good friends, Dwight?"

He didn't respond immediately.

After a moment, he said, "I reckon so."

Relief swept through her, and she hurried around the table. She grabbed Fran by the arm and smiled at her.

"You look absolutely ravishing, my dear. You simply must come and sit down with us. I know Dwight will want to find out all about you." She turned a big smile to him, desperate to make them both comfortable again. "Isn't that right? Why we will all have a good time together, the four of us."

Belinda was delighted to see the amusement on Fran's face. Her eyes shined at Belinda , and her lips twitched as she tried not to smile.

"Four of us?"

"Oh, I'm including Lionel." She laughed softly and tugged on Fran's arm to bring her over to the table. They went around it together, and she pulled out the chair opposite of hers. "Now, you just sit right down here. I'm going to tell Betty—that's the cook—that you've arrived and you need a plate assembled. Is there anything you cannot eat or don't like?"

Fran, still looking somewhat lost, shook her head. "No. I'll eat almost anything."

"Uh oh," Belinda laughed, turning her eyes to Dwight. "You're gonna have a new menu in the future, I think. I'll leave you two to talk, and I'll be right back with a plate for you, honey."

She flashed them a radiant smile. When her eyes settled on Dwight, she had to fight the tears that sprung to her eyes. She turned and hurried away before he could see. He had been *smiling* at her. She thought about it as she went to the kitchen door on the other side of the room and realized she had not seen a smile like that on his face since she arrived. She didn't even get a smile that big when she arrived. Not that she would have.

Dwight asked Fran to come. They had been corresponding. Not Dwight and Marie. He probably remembered every detail of Fran's letters to him. She felt like he would have had to really like Fran to ask her to come, especially during this troubled time.

She passed through the door to the kitchen and grinned wide at Betty, who gave her a contemplative look, one eyebrow raised. The woman ran her hands down her apron to clean them.

"What is that look for, young lady?" she asked.

"There's a woman here, Betty," Belinda replied. "And she is the one Dwight will marry. I can see it."

Betty blinked rapidly, an astonished look on her face.

"You are not the woman he was writing to?"

Belinda was taken aback by the question. She hadn't realized Betty knew about the mail order bride idea Dwight had used to find a bride.

"No. As a matter of fact, Lionel hired me to investigate the crimes the sheriff is trying to pin on Dwight. He believes in his friend's innocence. And so do I." She hesitated before asking. "I didn't know you knew about him placing an ad for a bride."

"Oh yes," Betty nodded when she spoke. "He told everyone on the staff."

"He told the ranch hands, too?"

"Yes, that's right. Everyone."

Belinda stood there for a moment before stammering that Fran needed a plate of food. If Mick knew about Dwight trying to find a bride, maybe that was what prompted him to commit crimes and pin them on Dwight?

It was a little farfetched. But it was plausible.

23

On the way to Big T, Lionel felt apprehensive. The last time he'd seen his friend, Dwight was about as down in the dumps as he could be. He wondered what Belinda would do to cheer him up. He hoped the two of them wouldn't fall in love. He didn't know how he would feel about it. He'd clearly seen that look returned to him when he'd caught her on the steps. Surely she had feelings for him, too.

His mood completely shifted when he emerged from the long pathway from the road and saw Belinda , Dwight, and another woman sitting on the porch. Belinda was talking animatedly. Dwight and the woman were looking directly at her, apparently enthralled by her words.

He almost didn't want to disturb them, but he was too curious. He wanted to know who the woman was and why Dwight had a smile on his face that had been missing for the last five years. The last time Lionel had seen his friend look like that was before Dwight even left Josephson County.

They were so entrenched in the conversation, they didn't notice when he rode to the stable and left Champion with Andy. He walked slowly from the stable, opening his ears to hear what Belinda was saying as he got closer.

"Larson and Sadie will be getting married this year, I think. Probably sooner than my other sisters. They are so good together. They really love each other so much."

"That's fascinating, Belinda ," the woman replied in an enthusiastic tone. "I can't imagine doing such stealthy and dangerous things. You must have such an exciting life."

"I really don't," Belinda responded. "It's my sisters that have all the adventures. This is the first time I've been on a case."

Chills erupted on Lionel's skin from his head to his toes. She had told Dwight. It must have been prompted by the arrival of the second woman. Lionel sorted through things in his mind and assumed that the woman was the *real* intended bride.

He was halfway up the steps before the three turned their heads and saw him. Belinda's face lit up, and she shot to her feet, sending a thrill of excitement through Lionel. She came around the table and passed the woman to hold her arms out to him.

"Here's Lionel," she cried out happily.

"Well, this is a nice reception. I think I'd like it a bit more often. What do you say?"

Dwight snorted. "You get enough positive attention, hero. Sit down."

Both men laughed while the women looked shocked. Belinda recovered first and pulled on Lionel's hand to take him back to the table. There was already a fourth chair available, and he took it. Before settling in the chair, he leaned forward, holding his hand out to the woman.

"Lionel Calverson."

She smiled at him and took his hand. She had a firm grip, and he liked her immediately because of that. And because of the smile she had apparently put back on his best friend's face. "Fran Lovern. I've been writing to Dwight for some time now. He invited me in a letter that he sent the day before Belinda arrived apparently."

"Is that so?" Lionel's face flushed as guilt swept through him.

"Oh, don't worry, Lionel," Dwight said, seeing the look on Lionel's face. "We've worked all through it. Fran and Belinda have made good friends already, and I completely understand why you did what you did, having her come here posing as a possible bride. She explained that she needed to get to know me without me being suspicious of her. Plus..." He moved his eyes from his friend to Belinda and then to Fran, "I've been going downhill in here..." He tapped his temple. "And her arrival was right on time. Lionel, you and Belinda are responsible for holding me up until now. From here on, you get to focus on yourselves and," He cleared his throat, "clearing my name."

Belinda and Lionel laughed softly together. When he caught her eye, he could see that look, the look he loved to see, deep in her eyes. He desperately wanted time alone with her.

"So we're working on a plan," Belinda said, "and you've come just in time to contribute."

Lionel raised his eyebrows, sweeping his eyes over his companions. He was impressed with Fran already. She was a pretty woman but not as pretty as Belinda. He thought he might be a little biased about that, though. She also seemed intelligent and easy-going, which would do Dwight a great deal of good. He was a tense man, internalizing most of his feelings. Lionel had a feeling Fran would bring out the best in his friend.

"I'm happy to do what I can. What's the latest development?"

"I've discovered from the cook, Betty, that everyone knew about Dwight's plan to find a bride through an ad." Belinda gave Lionel a direct look. "Even Mick. And as we know, Mick was supposed to get the ranch if Dwight didn't come back. Dwight and Fran are caught up on everything we know, Lionel. I've told them everything."

"All right," Lionel responded. "So it looks like we're going to have to catch Mick in the act."

"I don't know if you noticed, Lionel," Belinda continued, "but the pattern the lawyer pointed out to us showed that something is supposed to happen tonight. And if they stick to that pattern, it will be cattle theft. I propose one of us stays up late tonight, and when Mick leaves the bunkhouse—if he does— we follow him wherever he goes."

"I didn't notice, so good job spotting that," he replied. "I'll take the first watch if you want. How long are the shifts? I can only keep my eyes open for an hour or two. Then I really have to blink."

His friends laughed. Lionel thought the joke was quite stupid, but he was glad they laughed at it. It showed they really were his friends. Anyone else would have given him a strange look.

"I'll stay up with you," Belinda said, sending a thrill through him.

"I don't see why we can't all stay up," Fran said, surprising Lionel. It didn't take very long for the woman to fit herself right in.

Dwight nodded at the newcomer. "I agree. We'll all stay up. That way, when one of us is blinking, the others probably won't be. There will be eyes on him every second."

Laughter lifted into the air. Lionel felt a surge of intense relief, seeing Dwight moving swiftly back to the man he used to know.

"What do we do if he doesn't go anywhere?" Fran asked. "How will we know if he's even in the bunkhouse?"

Lionel raised his eyebrows, looking at Dwight. "The lady makes good points. I'll tell you what, I typically do a nightly patrol just before I leave for home. I've been doing that for a week or more because of the sabotage. Still haven't stopped it or seen anything, but I reckon that's because Mick just waited until I was done with the patrol and went out and sabotaged something on the land."

"Do you think he's working alone?" Belinda put in.

"That's a good question, too," Lionel responded. "I don't see how he could be. He has to have other men with him to steal cattle. He might be able to sabotage on his own, but he can't move a dozen head of cattle on his own. So how about if I look in the bunkhouse after my patrol, and I'll tell him and the other ranch hands to keep their eyes out for any suspicious behavior. You know they will say all right. Won't stop Mick from doing what he's doing."

"It's not very smart to leave a pattern when you're committing crimes," Fran remarked, moving her eyes to her companions.

"In my estimation, criminals are often not the smartest of men," Dwight observed.

24

Belinda watched through the window to see Lionel when he came from his patrol. He was in the bunkhouse right then, having gone to check for Mick and any cohorts he might have waiting to go out and steal some cattle.

She was in the parlor, sitting with her knees on the couch cushion, facing the window. Her eyes were on the bunkhouse right at that moment, wondering what was going on inside. Was he all right? Was Mick a dangerous man who had figured out that Lionel and Belinda had their eye on him?

Behind her, Fran and Dwight were having a low conversation, sitting together on another couch. When Belinda glanced over her shoulder at them, she was once again surprised by what an accepting man Dwight was. He had to be the most under-standing individual on the face of the planet. She was beginning to suspect it was his humble nature that irritated the mayor, the sheriff, and others, more than the fact that he hadn't been able to return before his father died.

They were jealous of him. He had an outstanding character, showing them naturally how flawed they were, how inherently weak they were as men. Dwight didn't even have to try. He was just like that.

She was incredibly glad to see him so quickly recover from the depression he'd been suffering from. He hadn't said it out loud, but she was sure that her arrival had thrown him for a loop. It was probably one of the driving factors for his depressed mood. He knew Fran was coming. He probably thought he would have to turn away the woman he had fallen in love with because another woman had intruded into his life without asking.

The relief when she confessed must have been tremendous for him. His behavior and lack of an angry reaction didn't stop the guilt from storing itself in Belinda's heart to be worked out over time. She had caused him pain without intending to. Now that things were set to right, she vowed never to do anything to hurt the man again.

It was Lionel she would be turning her attention to anyway. Not that she wanted to hurt *him*. She didn't want to hurt anyone.

Her thoughts were interrupted when she saw Lionel come out of the bunkhouse. He waved to the men inside and closed the door behind him as he went down the short four steps to the ground.

He looked up and saw her, lifting his chin one time in acknowledgment. She nodded at him and turned around, sitting right on the couch.

"He's on his way back. Mick is in there. I guess we'll be staying up late tonight."

THREE HOURS LATER, the clock struck one. The grandfather clock in the parlor bonged one time. Belinda was staring out the window at the bunkhouse. Her hour had just started.

To her utter relief, the door of the bunkhouse swung open. Tingles raced over her arms, and she spun around. "He's leaving," she hissed to the others. Fran was asleep, her body resting against Dwight, who was reading a book. Lionel was next to Belinda on the couch, but he was facing away from the window. They both got up and hurried to the other side of the room.

They'd kept the room dark, with just one lantern lit behind Dwight so he could see the words on the page. That was done so that when Mick came out of the bunkhouse, he wouldn't see the light and movement in the main house.

Dwight quietly woke Fran up and asked her if she wanted to come along or go upstairs to sleep. She was wide awake as soon as he shook her and said she wouldn't miss the adventure for the world, bringing smiles to the faces of her new friends.

Belinda hurried out into the foyer and went to the window to the right of the front door. She peered through, watching as Mick went to the stable, swinging his lantern casually as he went.

In preparation for the event, Dwight had rented three horses from a shop in town. That way, Mick wouldn't notice there were any missing. Lionel had moved Champion to the back of the house. If his horse had been there, it could have caused suspicion.

"Come on," Dwight hissed, waving his hand.

The four of them raced through the house to the back, where the horses and lanterns were waiting.

They had fashioned their lamps so that the light facing forward was blocked. They would only be able to see a few feet ahead of them, but they would easily spot Mick's lantern in front of them.

Once they were on their horses, they went around the side of the house that was furthest from the stable. Dwight moved to the edge and looked around cautiously.

"There he goes," he whisper-shouted over his shoulder to them. "He's taking the path around Liberty Pond. Doesn't that come out on Baker's land?"

"Yeah, but he's not a cattle rancher," Lionel answered.

Belinda was just there to follow the men. She was fairly certain she and Fran wouldn't be able to do much else. Neither had a gun, and she wasn't even close to a crack shot. She vowed at that moment to practice more.

"Well, come on. We know the trail. We can stay back far enough not to be seen and still come out at Baker's field to see where Mick goes from there. I'm glad he's alone. None of my hands are working against me. Just the foreman."

"Imagine that," Lionel said sarcastically.

The four moved over the field until they came to

the entrance of the trail to Baker's field. They could see Mick's lantern in the distance. After traveling behind him for ten minutes, they came out on the outskirts of Baker's field.

The four stopped as soon as they emerged from the woods. They saw a group of men approaching Mick.

"Oh my Lord," Dwight said under his breath. "It's Baker's men. Why are they doing this to me?"

"I doubt they are doing it to you, specifically, Dwight," Lionel responded. "They are in it for the money. I'm sure of that." He turned to Belinda , who was behind them, waiting with Fran. "We're gonna follow them to the ranch they're gonna steal from. As soon as we find out which one, I want you ladies to go to town and get the sheriff. He'll probably be at home. If you want to get the inspector, he will be at the boarding house."

"Okay," Belinda said, nodding. She glanced at Fran, who looked back at her and nodded, as well.

The four waited until the group of bandits went to the edge of the property before coming after them.

They traveled behind the group down a winding trail until they came to the Dunkirk's ranch.

"Wait a minute," Lionel said, his voice confused.

He turned to look at Belinda. She could barely see him in the soft light of their lanterns and the half-moon above. "Didn't they already hit the Dunkirk's? Another theft of their cattle, and they'll be hurting."

"It's a good thing we're here to stop it then," Belinda said. She turned her head to Fran. "Let's go get the sheriff. He's actually closer than you think. I hope he isn't involved in this. I don't know whether to get him or the inspector."

"I like the sheriff more," Lionel answered. "Go get him. He's not involved in this. If it's anyone..."

He stopped. Belinda figured he was going to mention his father.

She and Fran turned their horses, and the woman followed her as she galloped away from the bandits and their men.

"Are you sure we're doing the right thing?" Fran asked as they rode away. Belinda gave her a questioning look that the woman probably couldn't see in the dim light.

"What do you mean?" Belinda asked.

"I mean, will the sheriff help us? Is he on Dwight's side? Dwight has written to me many times about an encounter he's had with those men in town. It hurts him, the things they say. He's got a sensitive soul, and I just don't want him hurting anymore. I wanted to come to Big T a long time ago, but he didn't ask. I couldn't simply invite myself." She grinned wide. "Like some people do."

Belinda had to laugh. "Well, I'm glad he finally did, even if it crossed over when I came. In fact, I think it worked out just like it should. You're here now. He's going to be fine."

25

"I think you're just what Dwight needed," Belinda remarked as they rode through town. The sheriff's house was just ahead on the left. "That's where we're going," she said, pointing at it.

They rode up to the house, and both of them leaped out of the saddles, raising the dust when their boots hit the ground.

Belinda was at the top of the few steps in two strides. She crossed the short porch and yanked open the screen door. She pounded on the door and called out, "Sheriff! Sheriff!"

Fran was beside her when the sheriff, clothed in a long nightgown and a cap on his head, eyes looking swollen and puffy, yanked open the door.

"What do you want?" he grumbled, peering through his lids at them.

"There's a crime being committed right now," Belinda said hurriedly. "It's at the Dunkirk ranch."

It seemed to take a moment for the sheriff to comprehend what she was saying. He shook his head eventually and mumbled as he slowly closed the door, "They already got hit. Thieves aren't gonna go back."

"You have to listen to us, Sheriff," Belinda demanded hotly, putting out her hand and stopping the door from closing in their faces. The sheriff stared at her in surprise.

"I beg your pardon."

"The crime is taking place right now," Belinda snapped. "And you will be doing everyone in this town a disservice if you don't go out there and apprehend the criminals right now. The man behind the crimes is Dwight's foreman, Mick. That's why there were Big T clues left behind. They were framing him for the crimes, leaving clues behind. We followed him to Baker's field, where he was joined by other men. They all went to Dunkirk's farm, and they are stealing cattle *right now*."

The sheriff stared at them for another moment. Belinda let out a sharp gasp. "We don't have time for you to question this," she cried out, throwing her arms up in the air. "We have to go now."

"They can't move those cattle very quickly," the sheriff responded. "I know where Dunkirk is. You two go home. I'll go out there and check it out."

"I think we should come back with you," Belinda said. "We have to make sure everything is—"

"You can't make sure of anything," the sheriff snapped. "Leave this to the men, please. You just go back to Big T and wait for Dwight and Lionel to return."

"But what if you arrest them?" Belinda asked. "You need to understand that we followed Mick because this needs to stop. We wouldn't have brought it to your attention if Dwight was guilty. You and the rest of you men. You're judging him from your personal opinion. You judge him from the pain of your grief, and that isn't fair. He's never even had the chance to mourn his father because of the way he's been treated. You need to be fair-minded. A proper sheriff would be."

Belinda had surprised herself with her tirade.

The sheriff gave her a long look. "All right. That's enough from you, young lady. I am fair-minded. I will not arrest Dwight or Lionel. There. Does that satisfy you?"

Belinda nodded. She was still nervous, but she had to trust the sheriff. She had no choice.

The two women walked to the bottom of the steps when the sheriff disappeared back into his house.

"We're not going until he comes out and we see him leave on his horse," Belinda said firmly. She crossed her arms in front of her chest. Fran looked at her, nodded, and crossed her arms as well, a determined look on her slender, attractive face.

"Maybe we should just go back to the ranch anyway and tell the men the sheriff says he's on his way."

Belinda thought about Fran's suggestion. "I don't know. The sheriff might be right. What if we go back and we're seen, and we blow the whole thing? I don't want that to happen."

"You're right. That wouldn't be helpful at all."

The two women were quiet for a moment. Belinda moved her eyes to the woman, scanning her profile. "How long were you corresponding with Dwight?"

Fran seemed to think about it. "Well, I answered his ad about, I guess, six months ago."

"Six months ago?" Belinda questioned, "that's a really long time. I'm surprised he kept any of the other letters for Lionel to see them so I could get a name from one of them."

"He told me he had written to two other women a few weeks ago in a letter," Fran said. "He said he was writing them a final letter to tell them he'd made a choice, and that choice was me. He asked me to accept the train ticket inside, and he gave me a week to get my things in order. Now, I'm left wondering if he forgot that he'd sent the train ticket. If he'd forgotten about me altogether."

"No." Belinda was firm with her response. "He didn't forget about you. I've been harboring some guilt since you got here this morning because I think the knowledge that you were coming when I was already here was starting to really burden Dwight. I think he was incredibly relieved to realize that the woman he really loved wouldn't have to be turned away because someone else had usurped her position. I'll have you know that there was no intimacy between myself and Dwight. The only thing I did was hug him to comfort him when he was sad. And believe me, he was sad. I knew something was heavy on his mind, but I thought it was his father. I'm actually glad it was you, instead."

"I'm sure his father was still on his mind."

"Oh, yes, I know." Belinda nodded, moving her

eyes to the front door of the sheriff's house. He had yet to come out. She was beginning to get nervous. Was he going to let them down? Had he gone back to sleep? "But to know that one part of his burden was relieved and that you are here to help him with the other must be a tremendous relief for him."

"I am glad you see it that way. I'm glad that I didn't have my position usurped." She grinned wide. Belinda tilted her head, looking at the woman curiously.

"Are you making fun of me?" she asked with a big smile, lifting the octave of her voice higher.

"Oh no, not at all." The friendly smile on Fran's face did not waver. Belinda liked her more and more as time went on.

"I have to admit, I'm really curious about how this is going to happen. I think I'd like to be there when it does."

"I know," Belinda laughed when she spoke. "I feel the same way."

"Maybe we should just go and not wait for the sheriff?"

"I want to make sure he's coming first," Belinda replied, "but yes, let's go back to the Dunkirk ranch. The sheriff can't stop us." She looked up at the door again. "Where is he?" she asked anxiously.

As soon as she spoke the words, the man pulled open his door and stepped out. He was in his uniform, hat and all.

As soon as she saw him, she gestured with her head to Fran, and the two women hurried to their horses.

26

———

As soon as the women were gone, Lionel and Dwight moved their horses to the wooded area closest to the pasture where the cows were that the bandits were after. They watched from there, and Lionel took the time to pull out his pipe, pack it and light it.

"Terribly glad you got the woman you wanted, Dwight," Lionel said in a low voice. "Fran seems really great."

"She is," Dwight responded with a nod. "I've been writing to her for a really long time. I wanted to ask you, why did you pick Marie Wright? I had just written to her a month ago that I had made my choice and it wasn't her. I was polite. But when

Belinda showed up claiming to be her, I thought my letter must have gotten lost in the mail. For the entire week, I thought Belinda thought one letter from me meant an offer of marriage. I wrote to Marie, Ellen, and Fran. After corresponding with Fran for some time, I decided to write to the others and tell them about Fran. I had fallen in love with her through those letters."

"You must have been really upset to see Belinda." Lionel felt a pang of guilt. "I'm really sorry. That wasn't my intention. No wonder you were looking so stressed over everything. I didn't mean for that to happen."

"I know," Dwight replied. "Your heart was in the right place."

"It really was. I didn't know what else..." He let his words trail off, his eyes peering at the group of men in the distance as they rounded up a group of cows to drive out of the pasture. "Where's Mick?" he asked.

Dwight's head jerked toward the group of men in the distance. "I don't see him."

"Oh, no," Lionel groaned. "Where did he go?"

"Look. There he is."

Mick was riding away from the group, going

toward the house. Lionel and Dwight urged their horses through the woods, under cover of the trees and darkness, watching him closely. The foreman passed the Dunkirk's house.

"I can't believe no one inside hears these horses," Dwight said. "This is the second time they're being hit by these bandits."

"The Dunkirks are elderly, remember? Their son works the ranch. They are the only ones in there that would hear."

"Ah," Dwight nodded. "Well, he's not stopping there. We should follow him. The ladies will be back with the sheriff soon, I'm sure."

"We can't just let him run off," Lionel said in agreement.

Without another word, the two men followed the foreman as he left the Dunkirk property and headed toward town.

It didn't matter how dark it was. When Mick turned onto a road Lionel knew well, his heart sank into his stomach.

"What's going on?" Dwight asked, alarm in his voice.

They were heading toward the mayor's mansion.

Lionel had been hoping his father had nothing

to do with the crimes afflicting the county. But with Mick heading straight there, he had to believe it. The leader of the bandits wouldn't be going there if Jack wasn't involved.

"I think my father is the actual mastermind behind this." Lionel's voice came out tense. He couldn't help it. His entire body had stiffened with tension when Mick turned onto his street and headed toward his home. "I have nothing to do with it, Dwight. You have to believe me."

Dwight moved only his eyes in Lionel's direction. "You know I do. And I'm really sorry to hear your pa might be involved."

Lionel shook his head, his emotions running rampant inside him. "There is not might to it. Not now. Now I know it's true. I suspected before. I've been fighting with him about this since it all started, and he kept encouraging the sheriff to arrest you for it."

"I didn't know that. I didn't know he was doing that."

Lionel clenched his jaw together before he said, "I think this means the sheriff is more on your side than we thought."

"That's a good thing since the ladies have just gone to get him."

"They might go for the inspector instead."

Dwight snorted. "Haven't you met the man? It's like dealing with a weasel. He's a slippery, slimy sort. They won't go to him. The sheriff seems to take what Belinda says as truth."

Lionel raised his eyebrows. "Did he say that?"

Dwight nodded.

The two men became quiet as they followed Mick through the huge front garden of the mansion. The paths in the garden led to a small maze. In the center of the maze, which Lionel knew like the back of his hand, there was a bench where someone could sit and contemplate how in heaven's name they would find their way out of the maze.

They stopped their horses on the other side of a patch of tall bushes, dismounting. Mick was already heading into the maze. Lionel grumbled in his mind that when he owned the place, he would add more bushes and have the maze completely rearranged so that no one like Mick could walk through it freely. He didn't care if it took him a year to remember how to get out of it.

He and Dwight, who also knew the maze well, walked in with their lanterns.

They were close to the middle when they were able to stop. They could hear the voices of two men,

Mick and Jack, arguing a few rows over. Their voices carried through the maze walls as if they were echoed.

"You owe me, Jack," Mick was saying angrily. "You never paid up for the last batch of cattle we drove out and auctioned off. These men aren't gonna work if they're not paid. And I'm sure not doing it."

"You should have taken your pay out of the profit from selling the cattle," Jack retorted in a high and mighty voice. "That's what any other cattle rustler would have done. I thought you were the people who never trusted anyone. You've learned your lesson now, haven't you?"

"Look, Mayor," Mick's voice was sneering. Lionel could picture it on the man's face in his mind. "You're gonna pay up. There's lots of things that can happen if you don't. Those boys, most of them been travelers all their lives. You think there isn't a murderer among them?"

"You can't kill me," Jack responded hotly. "I'm the mayor. It wouldn't go unnoticed."

"You know what the thing about that is?" Mick asked. "You would be missed, that's true. But your son would also be missed when he is found guilty of your murder and hangs for it."

Lionel stiffened once more. How would his father respond? His heart thumped hard in his chest. He could feel Dwight's sympathetic eyes on him.

"You can't pin anything on my son," the mayor growled. "He's too smart. He'd figure it out long before you had a chance to convince anyone. He knows you set up Dwight."

Lionel and Dwight shared a shocked look. Jack knew everything that was going on. Had he been holding back information to shelter Lionel?

Lionel wanted badly to go around the bend and confront his father. Dwight slapped a hand on his shoulder, though, as soon as he made a move to do so. He looked at his friend, who held his lantern up next to his head.

"Don't," he whispered so low Lionel was basically reading his lips.

He refrained from going around and waved his hand at Dwight. They left the maze behind, and once there were outside of it, Lionel turned to Dwight and said, "We've got to get the sheriff to send a deputy over here to catch these two in action. It would be a lot more believable if one of them said they witnessed this meeting. And if they overheard what's being said."

"I don't know if we have enough time to make that happen," Dwight said urgently. "But we gotta try."

27

When Dwight and Lionel got back to the Dunkirk Ranch, they saw the ladies in the same spot they'd abandoned. But there was no need for the men to stay behind. They could see the sheriff and several deputies in the distance, just outside the pasture and up the field aways. They were capturing the bandits and had three men on horseback with their hands tied behind their backs.

The men hurried to the women, who saw them coming, and gave them big smiles.

"We wanted to watch the action," Fran explained. She and Belinda weren't on their horses, so the two men dismounted when they got to them. Dwight immediately wrapped his arms around Fran, holding her close. Lionel went directly to Belinda and did the same thing. When he pulled away, she was looking up at him with utter surprise written on her face.

"I'm so glad you're safe," he said quietly. "When all this is over, I need to talk to you. We need to have a serious discussion." He dropped his eyes to her lips, wishing he could kiss them right then and there. But he had to hold back. He hadn't even gotten her permission to hug her. He wasn't going to press his luck.

"I can't wait," she whispered softly, grinning.

"Why don't you and Fran go back to Big T and wait for us?" he said, still not letting her go.

"What? And miss all the action? Where is Dwight going?"

Lionel looked behind him. Dwight had gotten on his horse and was heading toward the sheriff.

"Oh, I've got to help him. The sheriff might still be holding a grudge."

"I think it'll be fine," Fran said, glancing at Belinda. Lionel wondered what thoughts were exchanged between the two ladies' eyes.

"He probably will," Belinda agreed. "But I think you should go after him, Dwight. I don't know why he—"

"I'll tell you later," Lionel responded quickly, releasing her and moving back to his horse. He hauled himself into the saddle. "You ladies head home. We'll catch you up when we get there."

He turned his horse and raced after Dwight. He didn't catch up until he was at the group of men being held by the deputies and sheriff. Dwight was already explaining the situation to the sheriff.

He stayed in his saddle, roaming around the group of bandits whose arms were behind their backs, looking into their faces. In a way, they were all responsible for the set-up, even though most of them probably knew nothing about it. Still, Lionel was going to hold them accountable for making his friend's life miserable for so long.

"Come on, Lionel," Dwight called out, waving one hand. The sheriff was going with them to the mansion, leaving his second deputy in charge.

Lionel raced after the two men, coming up beside them. The three men rode side-by-side to the mayor's mansion.

Lionel was glad to see Mick's horse was where the man had left it.

"You two stay here," the sheriff said, approaching the maze entrance.

"Uh, I don't think that's a good idea," Lionel said, holding one finger up in the air."

"Why not?" the sheriff asked.

"Because that's a maze," Lionel responded bluntly. "And I know it like the back of my hand. This was my father's mansion before he became mayor. I've been here all my life. It's only the mayor's mansion until my father is no longer mayor, which could be very soon. And even then, it will be my home."

The sheriff seemed to contemplate it for a moment. He finally nodded, saying, "I trust you, Lionel. You know I do."

"Then let me lead you through the maze. I don't want you to get lost."

"I can simply wait out here until they come out."

"My father and Mick might have gone in the house," Lionel pointed out.

The sheriff looked momentarily bereft. Finally, he waved his hand at Lionel. "All right. You can lead the way. You stay out here."

Dwight just laughed and went into the maze before the sheriff did.

"Don't yell at him," Lionel said quickly. "My father might hear you. Just let him go. This is mostly about him, anyway, isn't it?"

"I reckon you're right." The sheriff followed Dwight into the maze. He looked over his shoulder when he was in the first area of it. "Does he know where he's going?"

"Trust me, he does."

"I'll follow him then."

The three men went through the maze, and Dwight stopped at the same place they'd been before. Lionel was relieved to hear the two men still going at each other. It was like they hadn't even left. He and Dwight exchanged a surprised but happy look.

The sheriff stopped, holding up both hands as if he was the only one who heard the two men arguing.

"You've gotten away with this for six months."

Lionel thought the timing of their arrival was immaculate. The sheriff froze, looking somewhat amusing as he listened to the conversation.

"You seem to forget your place, Mick. You aren't in charge here. I am in charge. You work for me. You do what I tell you to do. You don't threaten my offspring unless you want to put your life on the line."

Lionel couldn't believe his ears. Was his father really threatening to murder the foreman? He had to take a step back and swallow hard, humiliated beyond belief. Dwight stepped over to him and slapped a comforting hand on his shoulder.

He looked up at his friend, shaking his head. He was sure his disappointment was clear on his face. Dwight's expression was understanding.

"I've had it with this, Mayor," the other man snapped back. They heard a struggle ensue, and the sheriff, along with Lionel and Dwight, darted around the corner to where the two men were wrestling with each other. Mick had his gun in his hand and was doing his best to aim it at the mayor's head.

"No, you don't," the sheriff cried out, jumping on Mick and jerking him away from the Mayor, who looked astonished. Jack immediately stepped away from the sheriff and the foreman, holding his hands up.

"He tried to shoot me. You saw him. Arrest him. Lock him in a cell."

"I plan to," the sheriff responded, pulling out a length of thin rope and tying it tightly around Mick's wrists behind the bandit's back.

Mick was apparently done with being quiet. He began to yell at the top of his lungs. "You're going down, Mayor. I've got enough to put you in jail for a long time. All they could do is take away your rank, and you'll be nothing. Nothing. And they're gonna. I'm gonna make sure of that." He was hopping on one foot as the sheriff tried to push him as far from the mayor as he could. He looked behind him over his shoulder, trying to meet eyes with the sheriff. "You know he's a kidnapper, don't you? You know he's guilty of way more than just cattle rustling. I can promise you that. All that sabotage? Remember the fire back ten years ago?"

"Shut up," the mayor was screaming. "You shut your mouth, you swine. You ignorant pig."

The sheriff jerked Mick by his arms and took him to Dwight. "Hold on to your man for me, would you? Here. If he tries to run, just shoot him."

Dwight pulled the gun from his holster and tapped it against Mick's back.

"It's a good thing the sheriff figured this out before I did."

Mick just sneered at Dwight, who shoved him toward the entrance of the section they were in. "You know your way back. Get going."

Mick stumbled forward but managed to keep himself on his feet. He and Dwight disappeared around the corner, and Lionel returned his eyes to the sheriff and his father.

The sheriff had approached the unsuspecting mayor, turned him around violently, and tied his wrists behind his back.

"You are also under arrest, Mayor Calverson. For multiple charges to be named later."

"You can't make anything stick on me, sheriff," Jack responded snidely. He glared at Lionel. "I reckon this was just what you were hoping for, wasn't it, boy?"

Lionel just shook his head, his heart breaking as the sheriff led his father out of the maze. At the entrance to the bench section, the sheriff pulled the mayor to a halt and looked over his shoulder at Lionel, who was behind them.

"I'm not trusting this fool to lead me out. Come on. Show me the way."

28

———

As Lionel led his father and the sheriff out of the maze, he denied how much it hurt that his father was responsible for so much destruction. Mick was still yelling out accusations a few minutes later when they emerged.

"You can't believe a thing this fool says," the mayor was bellowing.

The sheriff shoved the man forward so that he nearly collided with Mick.

"You two are going to be in cells right next to each other," he said with a snarl. "And if you argue the whole time, I have a few deputies that will know how to shut you up."

"You can't do this to me," the mayor roared in anger. "I am the mayor."

The sheriff frowned at him. "We all know that. Mayors can be criminals, too. And you are one of them." He turned his gaze to Lionel. "Would you mind if I used your buggy? I don't want to put these two on horseback."

"Not a problem. I'll go and get it right now."

Lionel headed off, leaving Dwight and the sheriff to keep the two men from bumping into each other roughly and kicking out at each other.

He swiftly brought the buggy back, happy that the harness was all ready to go. He drove the team back to the entrance of the maze and got down, leaving the reins over the front of the buggy.

"There you go, Sheriff."

He stepped back, letting Dwight lead Mick to the buggy and push him up into it. The grumbling had started, but fortunately, the yelling had stopped. The mayor was still in an uproar, but the sheriff stopped it by pulling out his gun and whacking the man over the head with it, knocking him unconscious.

Lionel hated to see that happen to his father, but the man had been causing a ruckus. He wasn't going to go quietly. That was obvious.

Lionel and Dwight went back to their horses and got up in the saddle. They hadn't even spoken a word to each other. It was as if they were of the same mind.

"Ready to go back to the women?" Dwight asked.

"I sure am."

"I take it you and Belinda are going to be a couple now?"

"You better believe it," Lionel responded with a nod.

"Listen, I'm here for you right now. I know what it's like to be without your father."

Lionel shook his head. "I don't think it's the same thing, Dwight."

They began to ride away from the mayor's mansion. "You had a loving relationship with your father. I didn't have anything like that with mine. I suspected he was involved already but didn't want to believe it. I'm sorry I didn't. I might have spared you some heartache."

Dwight tilted his head, staring out in front of him. "I don't think there was anything you could do more than you've done for me, Lionel. You've been a great friend to me."

"Even though I almost wrecked your future with Fran?"

Dwight laughed, which made Lionel feel a little better. "You didn't do that. I really think we would have worked it out somehow. Belinda knew what she was doing. She told me she'd thought about confessing almost right away. She only did it to see if she thought I was innocent. She decided I was the first day and almost told me that night. We'd had a good conversation, but I told her I was upset about my father. It was really because all I could think was that Fran was going to be coming on the train and I already had a woman there who claimed we were supposed to get married. I had no idea what I was going to do to get out of that."

"I really feel bad about putting you through that."

"It's all worked out in the end. Right now, I just want to get back to Big T, and to the woman I adore."

"Aw, ain't you sweet," Lionel teased. Dwight just gave him a look that made him laugh.

TWENTY MINUTES LATER, Dwight and Lionel were in the Big T Ranch parlor, snuggling up to their women.

In reality, they were just sitting next to the ladies on the two couches that faced each other with a coffee table in the middle. Belinda had prepared hot cocoa and made some small sandwiches that were so far untouched. Lionel didn't know about the others, but his stomach was still in knots. He didn't want anything to eat.

"I'm so glad things have turned out this way," Belinda said, leaning against Lionel with a cup between her hands. She took a sip, looking over the rim at Lionel as she took a drink.

"I feel the same way," Lionel said, nodding. "But I think if we all don't get some sleep soon, we're not going to be worth anything tomorrow."

"You silly man, the sun will be rising soon."

Lionel gave her a teasing look. "Is three hours soon to you?"

Belinda chuckled. "I always wake naturally at seven in the morning. If I sleep later, I will have a headache all day."

"I have some powders for that," Dwight responded. "I think we'll all need them in the morning."

"I don't even know if I can sleep," Belinda said.

Fran laughed softly. "Just let my head hit that pillow," she said. "I've been up almost twenty-four hours, and I'm not used to that. Even when I was taking care of babies as a nanny. I never had to stay up twenty-four hours. I'm exhausted."

"I better be getting back to the mansion," Lionel said, pushing himself to his feet.

"You aren't going back there tonight," Dwight responded, also standing up. "There's plenty of room here. I have guest rooms upon guest rooms. My father was never one to close his doors to those in need. And you need a good bed right now."

Lionel laughed. "You're right. Thanks, my friend."

Dwight looked at Fran. "I haven't even had time to show you to your room, have I? Come along. I think you'll like it. I designed it special for you. Your favorite colors and all that. Just for you."

"Oh, Dwight," Fran replied in a loving voice. "That is so nice of you."

"Anything for my lovely lady."

Lionel was stunned to see the difference the love of the right woman made for his friend. He looked down at Belinda , ready to offer his hand to help her up. He chuckled when he saw she had rested her head against the couch and her eyes were closed. "Belinda ," he said softly. "Belinda."

He gently placed his hands on her arms and shook her. She didn't wake.

He scooped her up into his arms. She rolled into

them easily, her head landing on his shoulder. She didn't even alter her breathing.

"She is really asleep," he remarked. "I'll take her up to her bed."

Dwight nodded. He and Fran let Lionel carry Belinda past them. He went up the stairs and had to wrestle with the doorknob with one hand before he finally got it to turn. He pushed the door open with his foot and went inside the dark, cool room.

There was just enough light coming through the window and the hallway lamps behind him to see her bed. He took her to it and laid her down gently, removing her shoes when she was out of his arms.

He set the shoes aside and began to maneuver the covers so he could get them out from under her without waking her.

Finally, when her covers were over her and she turned on her side to be comfortable, he leaned and kissed her lightly on the cheek.

"I'll see you in the morning, my love. Everything is going to be better now."

29

The sun was bright in the clear blue sky the next day when Belinda and Lionel joined Dwight and Fran on the veranda of the Big T Ranch. They were indulging in a feast for lunch. As soon as Belinda saw the layout on the long outdoor table, she thought about how hungry she was.

"I just realized I'm half-starved. I was too nervous to eat much last night and only picked at breakfast today."

"I noticed," Dwight remarked. "That's why this is here. None of us really ate well yesterday, did we?"

"You've been to the jailhouse, haven't you?" Lionel said, taking a seat near the food and leaning over to grab a banana, which he proceeded to peel.

Dwight nodded. "I have. My name has been cleared. Mick has spilled everything to the sheriff and the inspector."

"I bet they weren't too pleased to have been humiliated like that. Proven wrong," Fran observed.

"No, they weren't. But it didn't matter. I was vindicated. My name is cleared. At least of that."

"I don't think, after what has been discovered about the mayor, I don't think anyone will be holding anything against you anymore," Lionel said confidently.

Belinda listened to the two men talking, gazing at Lionel through loving eyes. Fran noticed and grinned wide at her friend. Belinda smiled back.

The men stopped talking, which got Belinda's attention. They were now looking at the women with curious eyes.

"So when do you plan to get married?" Belinda asked, her tone light and happy. Fran bit her bottom lip, looking over at Dwight with a secret smile on her face.

"I don't know. When were you planning on it, Dwight?"

Dwight looked contemplative. "I don't think we'll want to wait long. Maybe… I don't know six hours?"

Laughter rose into the air.

"Six hours?" Belinda remarked. "That doesn't give us long to prepare. She's still got to get a dress, and you have to get a preacher and—"

"I think he meant to say six *weeks*," Fran cut her off to say, her eyes on Dwight. "Isn't that what you meant to say?"

"As a matter of fact, it was." Dwight's reply was in the form of shock, but he abruptly laughed afterward. "Yes. Six weeks, it is. We'll have a confirmed date later when I talk to Pastor Edward."

"You can talk to him tomorrow at church," Lionel said.

"I'll do that."

"I think I'll be talking to him, too. I have an idea. I think I'll be getting married, as well, sometime soon."

Belinda's skin erupted in tingles. She was already looking at him with a smile, but her smile grew larger. "Is that right?" she asked.

"Yes." He looked around at the others. "It doesn't look like this is coming as much of a surprise to you. I wasn't preparing to go through the mail order bride ads, though."

"That's a good thing," Dwight said. "Sometimes, it can get strange."

They all laughed.

Lionel turned to Belinda. "I think I've found the love I was looking for. I wasn't really looking, though. I gotta say that. I really thought I'd be a bachelor all my life. But then again, I thought I'd be living in a mayor's mansion all my life."

"It wasn't a lifetime position," Dwight remarked. "Eventually, his corruption would have come out. Everyone would have known."

"You're probably right," Lionel nodded as he spoke. "Still, it just goes to show how just a short time can completely change everything." He turned his upper body toward Belinda and leaned on the armrest of the outdoor chair. "Would you like to go for a walk? There's a spot out back that you probably haven't seen. It's like God decided to put his own flower garden there. It's absolutely beautiful."

Belinda felt a measure of excitement slide through her. She nodded vigorously. "But first, I have to make a plate of food. I'm so hungry I could eat a horse."

"I don't recommend that," Dwight quipped, "I hear the meat is very tough."

"I don't even want to try it," Belinda said, picking up a plate from the table and walking down the length of it, putting items on it. Her stomach rumbled, so she put three grapes in her mouth and reveled in the taste.

Lionel put his arm around her shoulders, and the two walked side by side down the outside stairs that led to the backyard. Belinda had never been back there before. She hadn't even seen the back of the house except in the dark the night before when they'd gone out to follow Mick.

As they walked, she wondered if she should say anything about his father. Should she offer her condolences that the man turned out to be a criminal? She remembered seeing Lionel fighting with him in the office, and how devastated and broken Lionel looked afterward. She couldn't place whether that was just anger or if he was as hurt as it looked to her.

"I hope you know, Belinda ," he said when they were well away from the veranda and just a short walk to the path through the woods he was taking her to, "I was talking about marrying you back there."

Belinda grunted a chuckle. "I did think that, Lionel."

"Would you be willing to marry a bachelor like myself?" he asked humorously.

She narrowed her eyes, looking up at him. "I

think I could give it a try, at least."

He laughed, turning her to him with his hands on her shoulder. She nearly smashed the plate of food between them but lowered it so that wouldn't happen.

His grin stayed in place. "So you will marry me?"

"I will marry you, yes. But wait." She held up her hand between them when it looked like he was going to pull her to him. She turned and set the plate of food on the ground behind her. When she turned back, she held her hands out to the side and raised her eyebrows. "Now I'm ready."

With a delighted laugh, he pulled her into a hug tighter than any she'd ever experienced. She definitely wanted more of those hugs.

She wrapped her arms around him, thinking her life was finally complete.

"You know, you will have to meet my sisters when they all return."

"Yes, I've been thinking about that. Do you think they will like me?"

Belinda let out a laugh of her own. "Of course they will like you. You are wonderful."

"Aww. Sweet of you to say."

"I'm just wondering when you will get around to kissing me. I've been waiting and waiting and—"

He cut off her words, abruptly pulling her close and pressing his lips against hers. Her body erupted in tingles. She returned the kiss with as much love as she had in her soul, matching the depth of his.

She was breathless when they pulled apart.

"Oh, Lionel," she remarked, touching her lips with her fingers. They were tingling. She'd never been kissed by a man before. "I really enjoyed that," she said innocently. "Can we do that again?"

Lionel let out a pleased laugh. "We can certainly do that a lot more, especially after we're married. What do you say, about six weeks? We could have a double wedding."

Belinda shook her head. "No double wedding. Fran and I are going to want to have our own days. Maybe close together so we can plan them at the same time but not at the same time. I already threatened her future. I'm not going to take that day away from her, too."

Lionel gave her an affectionate look. "You are the most thoughtful woman I've ever met."

"Thank you, Lionel. That means a lot to me."

"I love you, Belinda."

Belinda's knees weakened, but fortunately, she was still in his arms, and he kept her from falling.

"I love you, too, Lionel. So very, very much."

EPILOGUE

Fran and Belinda ended up planning their weddings together. The men had little to do with it. Although Fran was grateful that Belinda had rejected a double wedding, she did think having it on the same day was a good idea. Belinda insisted that Dwight and Fran get married first. Well after their reception, she and Lionel would go through the ceremony and have their reception. That way, they could act as each other's bridesmaid and best man.

The day went wonderfully, with no missteps at either ceremony. The reception for Belinda and Lionel was held at the Big T Ranch. The ladies planned it so that the second reception would be a much bigger affair. They would celebrate both marriages then.

Belinda didn't get a chance to see her sisters and their men until the reception. They had not arrived in time to help her get ready, as she had to prepare before Fran's wedding when they weren't there. The only thing she did before her own ceremony was change her clothes.

The new couples arrived at Big T Ranch together after Belinda and Lionel's ceremony. The huge field in the back had been set up with decorations, including a huge overhead tent with no walls on the sides. It looked like a humungous umbrella.

Belinda spotted her sisters immediately. They were all standing together, talking, looking around with admiring eyes, holding drinks in their hands.

Belinda ran to them, breaking away from her husband. They spotted her when she was on her way to them and screamed so loud, their men flinched and shrunk away from them. Sadie, Amelia, and Josie ran toward her, and they met in the middle. Amelia, her oldest sister, was the first to reach her and wrapped her arms around her, completely enveloping her. Josie and Sadie brought up the sides, and the sisters all cried together,

"Belinda. I'm so happy for you." Adelaide cried

out as she hugged her sister. "So happy. Such a handsome man. Why, if I didn't have Cody, I would be so envious."

"Me, too," Josie and Sadie said at the same time. They all laughed at that implication and hugged each other again.

Belinda turned when she felt a hand on the small of her back that had become very familiar. She turned her head and looked over her shoulder up at her new husband.

"Lionel. This is Amelia, Sadie, and Josie. My sisters. These are their beaus. And those are Taylor's children. That's Taylor. And Cody. And Larson. He's the security I told you about. The children are Bella and Alex."

As she named off the people that had gathered around them, Lionel shook their hands, even bending to give a deep bow to little Bella, taking the six-year-old's hand and kissing the back of it.

"A fine little lady, you are. You'll grow up to be just like your auntie, won't you?"

"I will grow up to be like my mama," Bella answered precociously. Her eyes turned to Josie, who tilted her head to the side and gave the girl a sweet look.

"Oh, yes, of course. What was I thinking?" He

continued shaking hands, and the men broke off to have their own conversation while Belinda introduced Fran to her sisters.

They all took seats at a nearby table, holding their drinks in front of them. Their chairs were facing away from the table so leaning forward to see each other was not a problem.

"I was so surprised to hear the story behind you two becoming friends," Sadie said enthusiastically, smiling at Fran. "However did you find it in yourself to forgive our sister for her terrible behavior?"

If Sadie hadn't been smiling wide when she said it, Belinda was sure Fran would have taken it a different way. But Fran was an easy friend with a sympathetic and compassionate personality.

Fran shook her head. "When I found out that she was doing it to protect my Dwight, I couldn't do anything but forgive her. She's a good woman with a smart brain. I suppose you are all like that, aren't you?"

"We are a pack, that's for sure," Adelaide answered. She was holding a glass of white wine and held it out in front of her. "I think we should have our own little toast to our sister and her new friend, Fran. Two of the strongest, most loving women we know."

Fran grinned. "Am I supposed to hold up my glass to myself? I'm not clear how this works."

"I'll hold my glass up in a toast to you," Belinda replied. "And you hold yours up in a toast to me. How's that?"

"I like it."

All the women held their glasses up and clinked them against those that were nearest. They took a drink at the same time.

Belinda's sisters began conversing with Fran, drawing her into the conversation, asking her about her life before she came to Big T and what drove her to answer a mail order bride ad.

Belinda's mind began to wander. She'd heard Fran's story before and was familiar with it. She turned her eyes to look at her husband, who was near the counters that held food and beverages for their guests. Lionel was talking animatedly to Larson. She imagined the conversation in her mind being about the PI agency and how Lionel planned to help out and learn the trade. He had plenty of money to pour into the business, but Belinda had told him already it was flush and didn't need any monetary help.

So he must be offering his services. Since he was talking to Larson, she suspected he was saying he

would help with security. If there was one thing
Lionel could do, it was protect women. Belinda was
sure of that.

Love for her new husband filled her heart. She
let out a soft sigh.

At that moment, Lionel's eyes turned and caught
hers. He continued talking but let his eyes linger on
hers. A loving smile lifted the corners of his lips.

And he never stopped talking.

Belinda laughed.

At the beginning of her adventure, she had felt
like everything was going to change.

But that was then.

Now everything was going to change.

She could feel it.

Click here for more Blythe Carver books!

Sign up for the newsletter to be notified of new releases.

Click on link for
Newsletter
or put this in your browser window:

landing.mailerlite.com/webforms/landing/p6l2s1